Welcome to Texas

The big, filt~~[barcode: S0-ADU-266]~~ bar stool over and stepped toward Ferdie. The entire saloon went dead quiet. Corny could only watch his friend face certain death.

"I don't like you or your fancy-pants mouth," the man said, murder in his eyes. "You come into my town with your snake-oil Yankee ways and your blood money made off the sweat and toil of good God-fearin' Texans. An' you think you can make everything better by buyin' me a lousy drink?" He eyed Ferdie with murderous rage. "Anytime yer ready, tinhorn."

Ferdie couldn't move.

"I said draw, Yankee!" the man bellowed and went for his gun.

Before the young Easterner could even clear leather, two shots rang out, and the drunk man looked startled as two holes opened in his chest. Before he could voice his surprise, he hit the floor, dead.

Ferdie and Corny turned to see Skye Fargo twirling his gun into its holster. Ferdie hadn't even come close to drawing his. The Trailsman gave them the once-over, downed his whiskey, and shook his head with a chuckle.

"You ain't from around here, are you?"

THE
TRAILSMAN
#224

TEXAS
TINHORNS

by

Jon Sharpe

A SIGNET BOOK

SIGNET
Published by New American Library, a division of
Penguin Putnam Inc., 375 Hudson Street,
New York, New York 10014, U.S.A.
Penguin Books Ltd, 27 Wrights Lane,
London W8 5TZ, England
Penguin Books Australia Ltd, Ringwood,
Victoria, Australia
Penguin Books Canada Ltd, 10 Alcorn Avenue,
Toronto, Ontario, Canada M4V 3B2
Penguin Books (N.Z.) Ltd, 182–190 Wairau Road,
Auckland 10, New Zealand

Penguin Books Ltd, Registered Offices:
Harmondsworth, Middlesex, England

First published by Signet, an imprint of New American Library,
a division of Penguin Putnam Inc.

First Printing, June 2000
10 9 8 7 6 5 4 3 2 1

The Trailsman

Beginnings ... they bend the tree and they mark the man. Skye Fargo was born when he was eighteen. Terror was his midwife, vengeance his first cry. Killing spawned Skye Fargo, ruthless, cold-blooded murder. Out of the acrid smoke of gunpowder still hanging in the air, he rose, cried out a promise never forgotten.

The Trailsman they began to call him all across the West: searcher, scout, hunter, the man who could see where others only looked, his skills for hire but not his soul, the man who lived each day to the fullest, yet trailed each tomorrow. Skye Fargo, the Trailsman, the seeker who could take the wildness of a land and the wanting of a woman and make them his own.

Texas 1860—where young men were taught hard lessons about the merits of growing up quick, learning a fast draw, and keeping their heads down when the lead starts to fly. . . .

1

The ballroom of the Astor Hotel in New York City smelled like jasmine, expensive perfume, roses, gardenias, and rancid sweat. The combination of sour and sickening sweet scents made Ferdinand Bertram Wallingford I want to up-chuck the forty-dollar Delmonico's dinner into the nearest flowerpot. His wife of almost twenty-five years, Bridget, was off chatting with some pot-bellied dignitary from a country Wallingford had never heard of, and whose accent he couldn't understand. Damn foreigners, Wallingford thought; not only were they polluting this country, but a man couldn't make out a damn word they said. Of course, it never occurred to Wallingford that his ancestors had not long ago just gotten off the boat themselves.

But as long as Bridget was off talking to someone else, she couldn't nag him about their errant son, Ferdinand II.

And just where, the elder Wallingford pondered, was his only son and heir to the Wallingford empire? Wallingford snorted and pulled a bejeweled pocket watch out of his vest pocket. Half past nine and still no Ferdie Junior.

Wallingford was a robust, barrel-chested man of fifty who could chew up and devour a tough steak and tougher men with equal ease. He also had a short temper, and it was getting shorter by the minute. Wallingford hated these society functions his wife was always dragging him off to, insisting as she always did that mingling with the uppercrust was good for business. For his part, Wallingford, whose worth was well into the millions, would have rather preferred saloon-hopping to hobnobbing with a bunch of stuck-up stuffed shirts who swilled expensive champagne and blew cigar smoke in your face.

No, it was his son Ferdie who should have been here,

waltzing with all the plump, pink-cheeked debutantes. Lord knew, if proper etiquette didn't prohibit it, the elder Wallingford wouldn't have minded shaking his toes with some of these luscious young cuties, who were the daughters of some of the wealthiest men in America. Pretty young ladies who had attended Miss Agatha Porter's School for Young Ladies of Social Standing, Croton-on-the-Hudson, New York. For the past two years, they practiced balancing plates on their heads and learned to roll their r's and sip tea with their pinkies outstretched. They were prize young fillies just ripe for the first well-to-do stud to come along and propose marriage, like the pretty little young lady sitting in a corner, crying into a frilly lace hanky.

Her name was Prudence Emily Van Cleeve. Wallingford watched her as she softly wept. He had never felt so helpless in his life, and reminded himself for the tenth time that evening to strangle his son if and when the peckerhead chose to make an appearance at this, the first debutante's ball of the social season. The little ingrate was to be Miss Van Cleeve's escort for the evening. The younger Wallingford's conspicuous absence had undoubtedly been noted by the rich, influential fathers of these young ladies, and certainly by Prudence's father, Hubert Thompson Van Cleeve.

Van Cleeve owned, among other things, the Van Cleeve Maritime Company, one of the biggest ship building operations on the East Coast. Ferdie Junior's marriage was to be the ingredient that cemented Van Cleeve's ship-building empire to Wallingford's shipping firm, Wallingford Shipping, Inc. "We'll ship your goods to hell and back and in half the time," was the Wallingford motto. Their merger would create a monopoly to rival a dozen Vanderbilts and Carnegies.

But no, Ferdie Junior was about to dump the whole thing into the nearest commode by his recent hell-raising all over New York City, disappearing for days at a time and usually being escorted home to the family mansion on Gramercy Park by the police. Four years at Harvard, and Ferdie had barely squeaked by. Wallingford had had to spread a substantial amount of cash around—in the form of grants, of course—to get his errant son matriculated with some degree of honors. Hell, Wallingford now mused, he'd dropped enough money on the prestigious college to get half the damned high-toned joint named after him.

Now, some four months since graduation, Ferdie had been drinking and sowing enough wild oats to feed half a million horses. Reading those trashy Western dime novels and pulp magazines and thinking he was a cowboy, though the boy had never been any further west than Tenth Avenue.

"Let the boy be, he'll grow out of it," Bridget maintained, as only a mother could. Wallingford wasn't so certain. Spare the rod, spoil the child, the saying goes. Wallingford could go several better: *Use* the rod and the dumb bastard will do what he is told.

"Open a wound and you open the ears," Wallingford told Bridget, but thus far she'd successfully kept her husband from opening any wounds on her son.

But not anymore.

Bridget Wallingford finished chatting up the ambassador of Prussia and much like her husband, didn't understand a single word he said. She smiled and excused herself, making her way over to where Ferdinand was standing alone, squeezing an empty crystal cocktail glass. Her husband was at the boiling point, she knew from experience, his chest heaving like a stag at bay.

"You don't look pleased, Mr. Wallingford," Bridget said, smiling for the world to see. She was an attractive woman, firm of breast with hips that had expanded only an inch or so since marrying Ferdinand Wallingford and bearing him a fine, healthy boy. Further attempts at children had proven fruitless, unfortunately, and Bridget had lavished all her affections on Ferdie Junior.

"Indeed I'm not, Bridget," the elder Ferdinand snapped. "The boy promised me up and down he would be here, and he's nowhere to be seen."

"He'll be here, don't you worry," Bridget said. She was the daughter of a West Side saloon owner, a fetching strawberry blonde who'd turned down dozens of marriage proposals in favor of the young, strong ship's captain, Ferdinand Wallingford I, who was no doubt destined for bigger and better things.

"The boy's getting on my nerves," he said. "Even more than usual. Lord knows I've tolerated his craziness for months, but this—not showing up at the most important night of his life—is more than I can stand, and I can't stand it no more."

"*Any*more, dear husband," Bridget said. "Can't stand *any*more."

"Hell's bells, woman," Wallingford croaked. "I begged you to let me take a horsewhip to the boy. Forty lashes plus ten would have taught the boy some respect."

"Forty lashes plus nothing," Bridget said. "You will not lay a single finger on my son. He's a fine lad, not some lowlife salty dog on one of your schooners."

"He's making me look ridiculous, Bridget," Wallingford said. "And a man of my standing cannot afford to look ridiculous. You promised he'd be here, and I promised what I'd do if he wasn't."

"He'll be here, Ferdinand," she said. "He promised me he would. Don't you worry."

"I'm past worrying and well into what comes after," Wallingford said. "And what comes after is not something you'd care to stomach, woman."

"He's not acting alone, dear husband. He's got a partner-in-crime, don't you know."

"I do know," Wallingford said, "and my eyes can see that *his* father is no more pleased about it than I am."

He pointed to a tall, thin, white-haired man, who was immaculately dressed in an expensive silk suit, pacing back and forth on the ballroom balcony.

"I think you two boys need to talk," Bridget said. "You've put it off long enough."

Wallingford watched the white-haired man, who was obviously worried, and with good reason. He stopped in mid-step and looked down at Ferdinand Wallingford I, accusingly.

Their eyes locked on each other. Both nodded. The white-haired man was as fed up with the situation as Wallingford was. He grabbed two glasses of champagne from a passing waiter and went to meet the white-haired man halfway.

"Luck," Wallingford said.

"Luck," the white-haired man said.

They knocked back the expensive bubbly. Wallingford

looked at his glass, then threw it at the nearest wall where it tinkled into shards. The white-haired man grinned and did the same.

"It's Fisk, isn't it?" Wallingford asked.

"That's correct," Fisk said. "Hiram Cornelius Fisk, of Louisville, Kentucky."

"I've heard of you," Wallingford said. He extended his hand. Fisk took it. "Wallingford, Ferdinand Wallingford. A pleasure to meet you, sir."

"The pleasure has yet to be determined, Mr. Wallingford," Fisk said in return.

"Can't argue with that," Wallingford said, grabbing two more glasses of champagne from a passing waiter. He handed one to Fisk. "To your health, Mr. Fisk, and to the health of your son."

"Likewise, I'm sure, sir," Fisk said.

They drank and again smashed their glasses against the wall. A number of New York society snobs looked over and regarded the two men with displeasure.

"Our sons seem to be delinquent, Mr. Wallingford," Fisk said.

"Six months out of Harvard," Wallingford croaked, "and still behaving like babes in the woods."

"My boy seems to have inherited his late mother's mischievous streak," Fisk mused. "I thought an institution such as Harvard would tame him, but if anything, he's worse."

Wallingford said, "Care to belly up to the bar, Mr. Fisk?"

"I should be delighted," Fisk replied.

The two men went to the bar, trying to ignore the hushed, admonishing tones from New York City's upper-crust.

Fisk said to the bartender, "Two cognacs, please."

Wallingford, the truth be told, would have preferred bourbon; Fisk likewise would have killed for some fine single-malt scotch. Real men's whiskey was hard to come by at a debutante's ball. Instead, they had to content themselves with the bubbly French wines that tasted like horse piss, and expensive cognac served in wide, round glasses that were a pain in the butt to grasp.

Fisk swirled the cognac around in his snifter. "To your health, sir," Wallingford said, and tossed his back. Across the room, his wife, Bridget, watched and shook her head sadly. Her Ferdinand would never be fully accepted into high society, whose members thought little of him. Not that Ferdinand thought much of high society, either. Most of the fancy-pants men and saggy-bottomed society matrons came into their money the easy way—they inherited it. Ferdinand Bertram Wallingford I had earned his, chiseling out a shipping empire twenty-five years earlier, from one rotting schooner, some spit, and a lot of nerve.

Though he never ceased his tirades against New York's most idle rich, Wallingford knew a foot in society's door was also a hand in their wallets. For this reason alone he sent his son to Harvard and tolerated society functions such as this one.

"Frankly, I'm surprised we've never met," Fisk was saying now. "In view of the fact that our sons appear to be close friends."

"Your Cornelius had been to the house this past summer to visit," Wallingford said. "Seems like an amiable young chap. Often wondered what he sees in that blankethead son of mine."

"Make no mistake, Mr. Wallingford," Fisk said. "My Cornelius is no angel. He's been getting into trouble ever since his mother died several years ago. To be honest, I'm at my wit's end. I don't know what to do with him."

"I've been giving this some thought, Mr. Fisk," Wallingford said.

"Call me Hiram," Fisk said.

"I've been giving this some thought, Hiram," he said. "And—"

He was interrupted by a roaring crash that echoed throughout the hotel ballroom. Both men, along with everyone else, turned their heads to the double glass doors, which were being kicked in. Plate glass exploded, revealing two young men on horseback, their horses rearing up before charging through the smashed doors and into the ballroom.

The two horsemen whipped out pistols and started firing at the ceiling. Guests screamed and threw champagne glasses and plates filled with oysters and caviar into the air as they scrambled away.

Wallingford and Fisk watched in open-mouthed amazement as their sons, dressed like Western desperadoes, complete with ten-gallon hats, boots, spurs, and custom-made leather holsters, galloped through the party.

The guns, however, were the latest addition to their wardrobes.

"Dear God!" Fisk gasped.

"Shit on fire and save the matches!" Wallingford said.

Ferdinand II—Ferdie to his friends—was riding a sturdy mare and firing shots into the ceiling, sending chunks of brick, wood, and chandelier showering to the floor. Cornelius—Corny to his friends—was astride a sleek black bay. He, too, was shooting wildly. They were whooping and hollering and were doubtless well over three sheets to the wind.

A huge ice figure of a swan sat in the middle of the room, pink punch spouting from its mouth into a huge crystal bowl. Ferdie Wallingford took aim with his six-shooter and fired. The swan's head shattered in a hailstorm of ice chips. Corny Fisk trained his Colt on the punchbowl—a large, easy target—and pumped two shots into it. The bowl shattered and started raining punch inside the ballroom. Bejeweled fat ladies, diplomats, waiters, musicians and the cream of New York society curdled in fear and dived for cover. Pandemonium was now the order of the evening.

"Good shootin' hombre," Corny cried happily. He pumped two more shots and made the rest of the swam explode.

"Purty fair gunplay your ownself, Kid Corny," Ferdie said, spurring the horse harder than he should have. His was a city horse, not used to the cutting edge of round steel. The horse reared up and sent him flying backwards, where he crashed into the buffet table. Salad, cracked crab, and platters of delicacies scattered all over the ballroom. The remains of a roast turkey bounced off Ferdie's head followed by an apple that seconds before had been in the mouth of a suckling pig.

The horse trotted over to the huge marble fountain and started lapping up water. Corny quickly dismounted and ran to his friend, who was covered with dinner and dessert. Three feet away, Corny slipped on a slab of roast beef and fell face-first into a twelve-layer, white angel food cake.

"Damn," Corny muttered, wiping cake from his face.

"We seem to be having some trouble with food tonight,"

Ferdie said drunkenly. He shook his head, soggy lettuce flinging from his hair, and picked up a rolling bottle of champagne. He yanked the cork out unsteadily, hitting himself in the chin. He turned the bottle away and the expensive bubbly sprayed directly towards his friend's face. Corny opened his mouth to catch as much of it as he could.

"Sorry," Ferdie said. He guzzled down half the bottle and handed the rest to his friend. Corny polished it off and tossed the bottle away.

They belched simultaneously and looked around the room. People were huddling behind chairs and jammed into corners, quaking in fear. The ballroom was in shambles.

"You know what, Corny?" Ferdie said to his friend. "I think we may get in trouble for this."

"I think we're already in trouble," Corny said, watching the dozen or so blue-suited policemen start storming through the shattered ballroom doors, billy clubs drawn.

Pointing to Ferdie and Corny, one of the beefy Irish cops shouted, "THERE THEY ARE, BOYS," and New York's finest descended upon them.

As Wallingford watched, the mountain of policemen grabbed the two would-be desperadoes and jerked them to their feet; the cops' nightsticks were in position to pummel them into oatmeal if necessary.

Bridget came up beside her husband and said, alarmed, "Don't just stand there, Mr. Wallingford, go see to your son!"

"I can see him from here," Wallingford said, the trace of a smile on his lips. "And I'm liking every bit of it."

The cops had the boys surrounded by now, and for perhaps the first time in his life, Ferdie looked scared.

2

"Bail is set at five thousand dollars apiece," the judge, who looked to be well into his eighties, said with a clap of his gavel. "Can bail be made?"

"Yes, judge," said the elder Wallingford. He glanced sharply at his son, who sat on a bench handcuffed. Ferdie Junior didn't look anywhere near as ashamed as he should have. Mostly, he looked hungover.

"Bail can be set for my son as well, your honor," Hiram Fisk said.

"So be it," the judge barked and slapped the gavel down again. "The defendants will be remanded to the custody of their fathers until trial date." He slammed the gavel again. "Next case!"

A few minutes later, Ferdinand Wallingford I and Hiram Cornelius Fisk escorted their errant sons out of the lower-Manhattan courthouse. Neither man spoke to their sons, who followed dutifully a few steps behind their fathers. The boys tried to look contrite, but failed miserably.

"What now, Kid Ferdie?" Corny whispered to his friend.

"I'm studying on it," Ferdie said. He was a tall boy who most fortunately inherited his mother's good looks, instead of his father's heavy, blunt features.

Corny was four or so inches shorter than his friend and was downright skinny next to Ferdie's wiry but strong frame. Not that it mattered; he fancied himself a gunslinger, and size didn't count when a man lived by the gun. "I'm not sure, Ferdie, but I think we went too far this time," he said.

"Ain't a-feered, are you?"

"A-feered?" Corny asked. "What's that?"

"It's how they said 'afraid' out West, dumbhead," Ferdie laughed. "A real gunslinger would have known that."

They followed their fathers through the courthouse doors and out onto the street where two carriages awaited them, the doors held open by uniformed drivers. The bright morning sun struck the young men's bleary eyes, making them squint. They'd waited ten hours in a dank, gloomy cell before court opened that morning when their fathers could pay the necessary cash to secure their sons' release. Their cell mates had been the lowest form of humanity—rat-faced, bug-eyed, bloodthirsty scoundrels who looked capable of slitting a man's throat for the pennies in his pocket.

"What did we do that was so bad?" Ferdie whispered to his friend.

"Drank a lot of hooch, stole some horses from those two policemen, galloped through the ballroom of a dumb hotel and killed an ice turkey."

"The ice sculpture was a swan," Ferdie said.

"We also took a considerable piece out of the ceiling," Corny said. "What are you worried about? Our fathers can afford it."

"Yes, they can," Ferdie said. "The question is, can my backside?"

"Trust me," Corny said with a wink. "We'll get over."

Once outside, their fathers headed for their respective carriages. Before they parted company, Corny said, "So when do I see you again?"

"Do what your old man says and sit tight," Ferdie said. "I'll be in touch somehow."

Ferdinand Wallingford I heaved his bulk into the carriage and shifted over, making room for his son. Ferdie followed, climbing inside. His father barked some instructions at the driver and they took off down Centre Street.

Ferdie and his father traveled in silence for ten blocks or so until the elder Wallingford croaked, "Ten thousand dollars, that's what you cost me last night."

"Father?" Ferdie said. "Whatever do you—"

Ferdinand I reached over and slapped his son across the jaw as hard as he could.

"Don't sass me, boy," his father snapped. "I didn't sail

10

the seven seas for thirty years to let a schemin' little mud-fish like you make me look stupid."

"Slapping me is not going to help things," Ferdie said, his eyes locked on to his father's. "If you're going to punish me, then do it and get it over with."

"Oh, no," the elder Wallingford said. "You don't get off that easy. You cost me a lot of money, son. Five thousand for bail, three thousand to the hotel—my half of all the property you destroyed—and another two thousand to bribe the judge who would have been more than happy to let you and your little friend rot in prison."

The carriage clip-clopped down Broadway toward the Wallingford mansion in Gramercy Park.

"But Father," Ferdie pleaded. "Cornelius and I were just playing. We meant no serious harm."

Ferdinand I clenched his fists and tried to keep his temper under control. Only the thought of his hot-tempered wife, Bridget, kept him from kicking his son until he was dead. "You try my patience, boy, and delight in doing so," he said.

"Father," Ferdie said. "I admit I was a bit drunk, but—"

"But nothing!" Wallingford thundered. "You've proved to be worse than a boil on my ass, and I'm fed up to my eyebrows with your crap."

Ferdie Junior sank lower into the seat. He said, "Father, I—"

"Don't call me Father," Ferdinand I snapped. "Not if you plan to stay kin of mine. You've tested my good humor, boy, and then some."

He yanked several dog-eared magazines from inside his son's jacket pocket.

"Western Yarns," he read sounding thoroughly disgusted. He tossed the first pulp magazine out the carriage window.

"Romantic Tales of the West," he snorted, and threw a second publication away. "This is why I sent you to Harvard, so you could read this rubbish?"

"I like it," Ferdie said. "The untamed West, the last frontier where a man can still breathe free, a land of adventure . . ."

"What would you know about being a man, or adventure. Bah," Ferdinand I snorted, looking at the last pulp magazine. *Journals of a Texas Gunslinger.* He opened to the cover story and read out loud, "Ambush at Apache Flat: How I Fought Off One Hundred Redskins and Lived to Tell About It." The third magazine took residence with the first two somewhere on the muddy streets of Manhattan. "Pure piffle! You mean to tell me you actually believe that nonsense?"

"I guess some of it is exaggerated," Ferdie said. "And the rest are probably downright lies, but I enjoy reading them just the same." Ferdie reached into the vest pocket of his coat and pulled out another pulp, this one entitled, *Black Ear Pike, Scourge of the Frontier*. "Yes, Father, I read these cheap publications, not because I believe them, but because I'd like to believe them."

"Meaning what?" Wallingford I demanded.

"You act all impatient and wrathy with me, Father," Ferdie said, "but deep down you know why I've been so rebellious since I left Harvard."

Wallingford I opened the carriage door and spat, then slammed the door shut. "Since you seem to know what's running across my mind, boy, maybe you'd be so good as to share it with me."

"The 'Salty Son of the Seven Seas,' " Ferdie said. "That's what people call you. Mother, your friends, business associates, everyone."

"What of it?" Wallingford I asked.

"I'll tell you, Father," Ferdie said. "You have something that says who you are, the very thing that defines you. You ran away from home when you were thirteen and went to sea. When you were one year younger than I am now, you had command of your own vessel."

"The Lady Evangeline," Wallingford I said, smiling a little at the memory.

"Yes," Ferdie said. "And that's my point, Father. You had enough adventures for ten men. Singapore, Hong Kong, New Zealand. Hell, you saw half the world. And how many women were you with? I can't even imagine, but I'll bet it was a hell of a lot."

The elder Wallingford turned slightly red-faced at his son's bold question. "That's none of your damned business," he rasped, embarrassed by his son's statement, which Wallingford I failed to deny.

"It doesn't matter," Ferdie said. "The fact remains that

you did. That's a lot more than I've ever done. Don't you see, Father? I thirst for adventure, to see faraway places before I settle down to the lifetime of drudgery that you and Mother have so graciously provided for me."

"Adventure isn't all it's cracked up to be," Wallingford I mumbled. "The world is a dangerous place. I've got a scar for every port I docked in," he said. "Anyway, I did all that so you wouldn't have to."

"I'm grateful, Father," Ferdie said. "But I'd still like to have a little adventure while I'm young enough to enjoy it."

Wallingford I said nothing for a few moments. The only sound was the steady clip-clop of the horses on the cobblestone street. While the little snot that his wife called "son" had gnawed on his every nerve since coming home, he was beginning to see something in him that he liked, possibly even admired. He looked upon his son and smiled. Then after a slight hesitation he said, "I'll talk to Mr. Fisk. We'll see if you and your playmate can take the summer to have your fun."

"You will?" Ferdie asked eagerly.

"I don't imagine a month or two out West can hurt you any," Wallingford said. "Get all this craziness out of your system, have your little adventure. I'll even give you two thousand dollars to spend as you see fit. I would guess that Mr. Fisk will do the same."

The carriage pulled up in front of the Wallingford townhouse in Gramercy Park. The driver jerked the reins and brought the horses to a halt. He dutifully opened the door, and Wallingford I started climbing out.

"Go to Texas, play cowboy," he said, then turned back to his son. "But make no mistake. This is no reward for what you did last night, not by a country mile. And I'll expect you back here on September first, exactly two months from today, ready to settle down and marry a respectable young lady and someday take over the business when I pop off. But if you don't," Wallingford I said, tapping his cane against the carriage, "if you cause any more trouble and don't buckle down, not even the Texas Rangers will be able to keep me from ripping your head off."

Wallingford turned and briskly climbed the steps to the townhouse front door.

Ferdie could barely contain his excitement.

"Thank you, Father!" he gushed. "I won't let you down."

"See that you don't," he heard his father call over his shoulder as he disappeared into the house.

"Yee haw!" Ferdie cried out.

"Really, Pop?" Corny Fisk said. "You're sending me and Ferdie out West?"

Hiram Cornelius Fisk ladled more oatmeal into his bowl from the tureen on the long table. He said, "Cornelius, I have asked you not to call me Pop. A pop is a sound, not a human being. If you applied yourself to your studies, you would know that. Do we understand one another?"

"Sure, Pop," Corny said.

Fisk winced, gritting his teeth. Hives, the butler, tried to suppress a chuckle. Hives was a portly, mostly bald man who had virtually raised young Cornelius after the death of his mother. Despite the boy's penchant for raising a bit of hell now and then, Hives was quite fond of him. It was no wonder the boy was unwieldy, what with being an only child with no mother and a father who put in brief appearances at best. Fisk had always been impatient for his son to grow up, and when he finally did, Fisk grew even more impatient.

"You have precisely sixty days to pursue this insane dream of being a Texas cowboy, or whatever it is you read about in that trashy literature you litter the house with. Frankly, I'm quite disappointed that after four years at Harvard—at considerable expense, I might add—all you want to do is rope horses and ride cattle."

"It's the other way around, Po—sir," Corny said. "Harvard was alright. Kind of dull, though. And the other students were real snotnoses with starched collars and fancy airs. If it wasn't for Ferdie, I wouldn't have had any friends at all."

"And if it hadn't been for Ferdie, his father and I wouldn't have to bribe half the politicians in this city to turn the other cheek to your run-ins with the law."

"I apologize for that, sir," Corny said. "Ferdie and I—"

"Ferdie and I," Fisk said. "That's all I've been hearing for the last year. First, the two of you dressed like Indians and did a rain dance in the middle of Harvard Square during graduation ceremonies."

"It was a ghost dance, actually," Corny said.

His father wasn't even listening. "Then there was the time you put monogrammed handkerchiefs over your faces and attempted to rob a Second Avenue trolley with toy guns, telling everyone you were the James brothers."

"I don't know why anyone really believed us," Corny said. "We weren't serious."

"The police thought otherwise," Fisk said. "But last night at the Astor, that was the icing on the cake, the cork out of the bottle. Shooting up the ballroom and scaring two hundred people half to death. Where did you get those guns, anyway?"

"From the Sears-Roebuck catalog," Corny said.

"I suppose that's where you acquired most of that ridiculous Western attire," Fisk said.

"Boots, chaps, blue jeans," Corny said, showing off his wardrobe, unchanged for two days. "Everything. The Sears people are very good."

Fisk wiped his mouth with a cloth napkin and rose from the table. He pulled a cigar from a box on the table and lit it.

"Hives, my hat, please."

"Yes, sir," Hives said, and disappeared from the dining room.

Fisk pulled a purse from the breast pocket of his jacket and removed a sheaf of green bills. He let them drop to the table. "This is for you. Two thousand dollars. Spend it wisely. I don't want to see your face all summer, nor, I suspect, do you want to see mine. Today is the seventeenth of June. I'll expect you at your desk and ready for work the morning of September first, at eight a.m. Until then your life is yours, and yours alone."

"September first, you say?" Corny asked.

"Correct," his father replied. "If not, you will no longer be counted as a member of the Fisk family. I'll cut you off like a diseased appendage." He jammed his cigar into an ashtray, snuffing the life from it. "Do you understand?"

Corny met his father's icy glare, but quickly looked away.

"Maybe I won't want to come back," Corny said.

"You'll be back," his father said. "Unless you're pigheaded enough to believe all the tripe you've been reading and get yourself killed."

Hives reappeared with Fisk's bowler and overcoat. Fisk flipped the hat on his head, then Hives helped him into the coat.

"I know I haven't been the most attentive of fathers to you, Cornelius," Fisk said. "And I suppose it's no fault of yours that your mother decided to depart this earth as soon as she did. This notwithstanding, there's a business to be run, a name to live up to. The name of Fisk, one that dates back to the birth of this country. And one that will continue to live long after our bones are in the ground."

He made his way out of the dining room, then turned back to his son.

"It's time to grow up, Cornelius," Fisk said to his son. "I strongly suspect you'll make an excellent adult. See that you do, and never forget that you are a Fisk."

Like you'll ever let me forget it, Corny thought. "Yes, Father," he said.

"Good day, son," Fisk said. "And don't forget to exercise great caution when you get west of the Mississippi River. The West's idea of civilization is quite different from your world here in New York. Expect the worst from people and your chances of survival will be much improved."

Fisk vanished into the gloom of the cavernous hallway. Corny heard the front door open and close with a muffled boom.

Hives broke the silence. He said, "Shall we pack your suitcase. Master Cornelius?"

Corny shrugged. He said, "I reckon."

Hives placed two dozen pairs of socks into the suitcase. He turned back to the chest of drawers and selected undershirts. Corny removed the socks and replaced them with a sack of Western story magazines. Hives removed the magazines, replacing them with the socks, then added the undershirts. Corny put the magazines back.

Hives said, "I do believe you'll be needing these more, Master Cornelius." He returned the socks and undershirts to the suitcase.

"Nobody wears undershirts out West," Corny protested. He sat on the edge of the bed and started spit-shining his boots and missing, splattering saliva on the floor.

"Then won't it be exciting to be the first who does,"

Hives said. He plucked three pairs of rumpled blue jeans off the floor and started folding them.

"Blue jeans," Hives sniffed. "An astonishing achievement."

"We call them Levi's," Corny said. "After their inventor, Levi Strauss."

"Indeed," Hives said.

Ferdie sighed deeply. "What a curious thing to say," he said.

"What, young sir?" Hives asked.

"What my father said, about expecting the worst in people," Corny said. "Not a very nice thing to say."

"What I believe your father meant," Hives said, "is that the West is a harsh land filled with harsh people. He's naturally concerned, young sir, about the conspicuous lack of law and order on the American frontier."

Corny said, "The West isn't nearly as dangerous as us Yankees think. Not anymore."

Hives carefully folded the blue jeans and placed them in the suitcase. He said, "As an Englishman, perhaps my perception of America is different from yours, Master Cornelius, and what I see and read in the newspapers leads me to believe the West is not nearly as charitable as you think."

"I guess . . . I mean, I *reckon,* I'll find out," Corny said. "Who knows, I may even like it there and want to stay forever. I might as well. My father doesn't seem to want me around." Corny paused and added, "I don't think he likes me very much."

"Oh, on the contrary, young sir," Hives said. "I believe your father is actually quite fond of you. You're confusing like and love, Master Cornelius."

Corny looked up from shining his boots, "I am?"

"I believe the problem is that it hurts him to see you making what he sees as a debacle of your life," Hives said. "Perhaps because he expects so much in himself, he has no choice but to expect the same in you. Fathers are like that."

"They sure are," Corny said.

"His giving you this summer for your own is his way of showing affection, I do believe, young sir," Hives said.

"Indeed, I reckon," Corny said.

Shots from outside pierced the early morning buzz of the

17

city street. Corny dashed to a window that faced the street, and flung it open. Ferdie was standing on the sidewalk in front of a livery carriage, firing his six-guns into the air. Businessmen, delivery boys, nannies pushing baby carriages, and several policemen all dived for cover.

"Yee-haw!" Corny cried out the window.

"Guess you heard what our daddies decided, partner," Ferdie shouted back. "Told you I'd work it all out!"

"Never doubted you for a moment, buckaroo," Corny said.

"Then hurry up and get your moss-covered ass down here and let's cut some sun while the hay shines."

"I think you mean, cut some hay while the moon shines," Corny corrected.

"Hey, look at this," Ferdie said, attempting poorly to twirl his pistol like a genuine Texas gunslinger. After missing twice, he holstered his pistol. He fished a silver dollar from the pocket of his blue jeans. "I been practicing all night." He tossed the silver dollar high into the air, pulled his Colt, aimed, and squeezed off one shot.

The silver dollar clinked onto the sidewalk ten feet away. Half a second later, a dead pigeon plopped to the sidewalk at Ferdie's feet. Feathers floated softly down after it.

"Good shootin', pard," Corny said.

"Never could abide pigeons anyway," Ferdie said a bit sheepishly.

"I'll be down in a Texas minute," Corny said, repeating a phrase he'd read in a book.

He turned from the window and returned to his suitcase, where Hives was rearranging his drawers.

"Real cowboys don't wear drawers, Hives," Corny complained.

"Seeing as how you'll be clad in those stiff, harsh pants from Mr. Strauss," Hives said, "I strongly recommend you do, unless you prefer to chafe your private parts raw."

Corny shifted uncomfortably, already feeling the discomfort of the new blue jeans he was wearing. "Now that you mention it," he said, "maybe you're right."

"Thank you, young sir," Hive said, neatly arranging the last of Corny's wardrobe. Corny went into the closet and pulled a big white box down from the top shelf. He plunked it onto the bed and pulled out a dandy white Stetson. He put it on, where it sank halfway down his forehead, like a rock in quicksand, folding his ears in half.

"I bought it at Epstein's Chapeau Emporium," Corny said. "It's called a ten-gallon hat."

Hives studied him for a moment. He said, "I think five gallons would have sufficed, young sir."

"The clerk said I'd grow into it," Corny said.

"Indeed," Hives said.

Corny pulled the suitcase off the bed and put on his jacket. Then he wiped his hand on his pants and stuck it out to Hives.

"Well," he said. "Guess I better be gettin' on."

"Indeed you should," Hives said and shook Corny's hand.

"Reckon I'll be seeing you in September," Corny said.

He'd never been away from home for more than a few weeks at a time, except for his years at Harvard, which was a short eight-hour train ride away. Saying farewell to Hives was much harder than saying it to his own father. Not surprising though, since Hives had been a much more familiar presence in Corny's life since childhood.

"You will if you proceed with caution, young Cornelius," Hives said. "Where is your firearm?"

"The police took it," Corny said. "I figured I'd get another when I got to where I was going."

"I think not," Hives said. He unbuttoned his suit jacket. Tucked inside his gray pants was a pearl-handled Colt revolver. He pulled it out and handed it to Corny.

"It's best to be prepared for all of life's unexpected twists," Hives said. "My present to you, young Cornelius. And may you never have to use it."

Corny, wide-eyed, clutched the gun admiringly. "This is great, Hives. How did—"

"Suffice it to say that your father often discusses with me his parental dilemmas," Hives said. "Sometimes I advise him on solutions. In other words, young sir, I knew you would be leaving."

"You've always . . . well, you know what you've been to me." Corny struggled for the words. "I'm obliged to you is all I'm tryin' to say."

"Thank you, sir," Hives said. "I suppose you'd better get moving. Your companion, Mr. Wallingford, is waiting."

Corny nodded, wanting to say more to Hives. He wanted to thank him for playing hide-and-seek with him when he was four years old, the night his mother died; thank him for being in the right place at the right time for as long as Corny could remember.

"I guess he is," Corny said, and grabbed his suitcase. Hives took it from him and said, "Allow me, Mr. Fisk." Hives smiled for what Corny thought might have been the first time.

Corny followed Hives out the door. At the top of the stairs, Hives turned and asked, "And just what is your final destination?"

Corny stopped. "I'm not sure I know," he said.

"Perhaps you'd better check with your friend," Hives suggested.

Corny went back into the bedroom and threw open the window.

He called to Ferdie, "Hey, partner, where are we going?"

Ferdie, who had been inspecting the chamber of his gun, looked up and said, "Texas. I've been doing some reading on the subject. There's not too much of the real West left, but I think we can find some in West Texas. There's a town called San Angelo. Has a nice ring to it—thought we could give it a try."

Corny closed the window and ran back to Hives. "A town in West Texas," Corny said, "called San Angelo."

Hives shuddered at this bit of news. He started down the stairs.

"San Angelo," Hives said, rolling his eyes. "West Texas. Indeed."

3

"Whiskey," Fargo said to the bartender. "And leave the bottle."

The sour-faced bartender slammed the bottle of whiskey on the bar and snatched up Fargo's silver dollar. His last, as luck would have it. He'd just come off a twelve-hour poker game upstairs in Slim Whitmore's saloon and had dropped everything he had, almost five hundred dollars.

Fargo had been kicking around San Angelo for a few weeks, having finally gunned down a particular nasty little killer named Billy Batts, a Louisiana lowlife who'd slaughtered several families in Texas and New Mexico Territory. Batts was a scurvy scum who'd just as soon slit a child's throat as squash a mosquito on his arm. The reward for his capture—preferably dead rather than alive—had swelled to a thousand dollars after Batts had slaughtered a rancher and his family near El Paso. Then Fargo caught up with him.

The thousand dollars was gone. Fargo had already squandered it on whiskey and women and clean sheets and some solid meals and gambling.

Fargo sipped his whiskey and watched the two young guys down at the end of the bar, tinhorns both and no mistake. They were laughing too loud, paying for everyone's drinks for no reason, and enjoying themselves far too much. In West Texas, fun was always in short supply. Men drank for anything but.

"Another round on the us, innkeeper," the taller of the two called out.

While there were a couple of takers to the boys' offer of a round, they were looked at with distrust by the majority of customers: grizzled, sun-baked West Texans who were suspicious of their own noses. They didn't cotton to strangers, especially ones with flat-toned Eastern accents, boots that were too shiny new, and britches with no dirt on them.

"Drink up, boys," the shorter of the pair squealed as the bartender poured brown rotgut into shot glasses up and down the bar. The shorter tinhorn was slapping the drinkers on the back cheerfully. None responded with more than an annoyed nod or grunt.

The bartender tilted the bottle to pour a shot into an empty glass. Before the shotglass stood a tall, stocky, unshaven man with teeth brown from chewing tobacco and about a month's worth of trail dust covering him from head to toe.

The man put a callused, beefy hand over the shot glass, and the bartender poured booze all over the man's knuckles.

Fargo watched, knowing what was coming.

When a man was looking hard enough for a fight, odds were good he'd find one.

"I can pay fer my own whiskey," the big man growled, not looking up but making sure the two tinhorns could hear him.

He shook the whiskey from his hand and said, louder this time, "And I sure as shit don't take no drinks from any Eastern peckerwoods."

The challenge, undoubtedly, was now officially thrown down.

The two tinhorns, Fargo saw, seemed uncertain how to respond. The shorter one walked back to his friend. They started talking softly to each other. Fargo could hear most of it.

"I think we've just been insulted," the shorter one said. "I didn't understand all his words, but the ones I did weren't very nice.

"No, they weren't," the taller one said.

"Do you have any ideas on how we should handle this?" the shorter one asked.

"Remember that book we read, *Shoot-out at Snake Gulch*?" the tall one said. "Remember what Hardcase McCoy did in the Fancy Lady Saloon?"

"Didn't he—" the short one started.

"—kill the desperado," the tall one finished. He was

22

smiling, looking kind of dreamy as he remembered. "It was in a place just like this, Corny. Hardcase McCoy draws his Colt and pumps three shots into the guy's head."

"That was a book, Ferdie," the shorter one said. "This is real."

The taller tinhorn, Ferdie, having decided he'd just been slighted, was glaring at the stocky stranger now.

He said, "Hardcase McCoy wasn't afraid of anyone, and neither am I."

"Ferdie, I don't think—"

Ferdie ignored Corny and walked out into the middle of the floor. Fargo sighed tiredly and put his drink back on the bar. This kid was even dumber than he looked.

New spurs clanging, the Easterner brushed the tips of his fingers over the butts of his pistols—which had yet to be fired, Fargo knew instinctively—and said, "Don't believe I like your subtext of hostility, stranger."

Fargo groaned. Either this kid had a death wish or he actually believed he could out-draw the stocky man. The kid would go belly up with a half-pound of lead in his gut.

The big man grabbed his empty shot glass and flung it away, where it narrowly missed some poker players at a table. He turned toward Ferdie, ready and eager to ventilate the skinny young bastard.

He kicked a bar stool over and took some steps toward Ferdie. The place got quiet enough to hear a rattlesnake fart.

The shorter guy was quaking in his boots, watching his friend walking into certain death.

"I don't like you or your fancy-ass words," the stranger said, murder in his gray eyes. "You come into my town with your snake-oil Yankee ways, and your blood money made off the sweat and toil of good God-fearin' Texans. An' you think you can make it better by buyin' me a lousy drink?" He eyed Ferdie with murderous rage. "Anytime yer ready to settle the score, you go fer it."

The smaller guy suddenly got his dander up and darted over to the stranger. He said, "The seriousness of your claims is not in dispute here, sir—"

The stranger shoved Corny aside, and Corny went flying into the piano player, sending them both crashing to the sawdust-covered floor.

"Draw, you Yankee bastard," the stranger said, and went for his gun.

Fargo took over. Before the tall tinhorn could even clear leather, Fargo was firing at the stranger. Two shots rang out and the stranger, in mid draw, looked startled as two holes opened in his chest. Before he could react further, he dropped his pistol and fell back against the bar. He slumped to the floor, his eyes staying open in surprise even as death washed over him.

Fargo twirled his Colt into his holster. Ferdie was still clutching the butt of his gun, never having even drawn his weapon, staring at the dead man in shock.

"D-did I do that?" he asked no one in particular.

"No," Corny said, still laying on the floor. "It was him."

He pointed to Fargo, who was turning back to the bar. Ferdie gawked at Fargo, who was pouring himself a shot.

He glanced down at the big stranger's lifeless body, which was already drawing flies. Ferdie had never actually seen a real dead person. And this guy was definitely dead. Only when saliva began dribbling down his chin did Ferdie realize that his mouth was hanging open in amazement.

Corny, still flat on his butt, likewise stared at the lifeless form sprawled on the dusty bar room floor.

"Do I know you, stranger?" Ferdie asked.

"Name's Fargo, Skye Fargo," he said, "but you can call me Hardcase McCoy if you're of a mind to."

"I didn't need your help, Mr. Fargo," Ferdie said.

"Yes, you did," Fargo replied, turning away from the boys to concentrate on his drink.

Corny scrambled to his feet, leaving the piano player flat on his back. Corny rushed over to his friend. "Are you all right, Ferdie?" he asked.

Ferdie ignored him. He said to Fargo, "I could have taken him."

"The hell you say," Fargo said, sipping his whiskey. "Gunslingin' don't afford you no second chance. Your dead friend over there had you hands down."

"You say—" Ferdie snapped. "I'm greased lightening with a gun."

"You couldn't grease your own pecker with a pound of Limburger cheese," Fargo said.

Fargo saw a look of anger cross the young Yankee's face.

24

He opened his mouth to speak, but his friend grabbed him and said to Fargo, "Don't pay him any of your mind, sir. We appreciate what you did."

Ferdie jerked his arm free. He said to Fargo, "I didn't need you fighting my battles."

"Ferdie," the shorter one said. "He saved your bacon. That man would've killed you."

"I was doing fine till he came along," Ferdie said angrily, kicking at the sawdust like a pissy little boy. Fargo sipped his whiskey nonchalantly.

"Can we buy you a drink, mister?" the shorter guy asked. "A bottle if you want it."

"A bottle?" Ferdie asked indignantly. "You want to buy this man a bottle? After he stole my kill? Are you crazy, Corny?"

Fargo finished the last of his whiskey and turned to the two young men.

"No thanks," he said to Corny. "I've had enough for now. But I don't think you have."

He hitched up his pants and wiped his mouth with his sleeve. He sauntered over to the swinging bar doors, and said to them, "You best come with me now, boys. We got some things to discuss."

"What things?" Ferdie wanted to know.

"Like how to stay alive," Fargo said. "I'll be over at the cafe whenever you're ready."

He disappeared out the door. Ferdie turned to the bartender and said, "Who is that man?"

"You heard," the bartender said. "Skye Fargo. And if you boys have half a brain between ya, y'all will get your asses over to the cafe."

Corny looked at his friend and said, "I do believe he's right, Ferdie."

Ferdie said, "Whose side are you on, anyway?"

"Yours," Corny said, grabbing his friend's arm and dragging him out of the saloon.

4

"You two ain't from around here, are you?" Fargo said to them, wiping up the last of the beef-stew gravy with a crust of bread.

"No, we're not," Corny said. "How'd you know?"

"My guess would be New York, maybe Baltimore, maybe Philadelphia," Fargo said. "But if I had to, I'd put my money on New York."

"You're very observant, Mr. Fargo," Ferdie said. "New York is correct."

"I thought so," Fargo said.

"What gave us away?" Corny wanted to know.

"The way you walk, the way you talk, the way you don't seem to know your asses from your toenails."

An aging, white-haired woman came doddering over to the table carrying a tray. On it was one solitary cup of coffee, which she plopped down in front of Fargo, sloshing some onto his lap. She tossed the battered tray onto a table and said to Ferdie and Corny, "You boys want somethin' to eat or are you here to feast on my beauty?"

"What kind of seafood does this establishment offer?" Corny asked her. "Can I get some sautéed blue snapper?"

"I can give you fried catfish, fried beefsteak, and chili and stew," the old gal said.

"Bring 'em two blueplate specials, Miranda," Fargo said to her, wiping coffee from his lap with a napkin. "And put them on my tab."

"If you say so," Miranda said wearily, and shuffled back to the kitchen.

"What exactly is a blueplate special?" Ferdie asked.

"After you eat it, you turn blue," Fargo said.

"Why did you help us, Mr. Fargo?" the short guy, Corny, asked. "We didn't ask for your help."

"You didn't have to," Fargo said. "But you needed it all the same." He sipped his coffee. "Do I speak the truth?"

"I think maybe you do," Corny said. "We're new to these parts."

Fargo said, "The question is, why are you here?"

"Why shouldn't we be here?" Ferdie asked somewhat testily.

" 'Cause you both stick out like a skunk in whorehouse," Fargo said to them. "Let me guess: you both are a couple of Eastern dudes who've read too many books and believe the slop those Yankee hacks pour onto the page. Let me set you fellers straight: what those writers say rarely ever happens, and when it does, they're never around to see."

Ferdie and Corny looked at each other, uncertain.

"Supposing you're correct, Fargo," Ferdie said. "Then what?"

Miranda toddled out of the steamy kitchen carrying a tray with two plates on it. She set them down on the table before the Yankees. The aroma of burnt pork chops wafted up at them.

"Then nothing," Fargo said. "If you boys got an ounce of smarts, you'll hightail it back to the bosom of your families. A smart sheep never strays far from the flock."

"We have money," Ferdie said, taking a stab at the pork chop. The fork bounced off. "Lots of it."

"Never knew a bankroll that could stop a bullet," Fargo said.

"What I meant was," Ferdie said, "you look like someone who can teach us everything we need to know about being real men of the West."

Corny nodded in agreement and said, "That's right, Mr. Fargo. You could teach us how to shoot, and ride a horse, and lasso a steer and chew tobacco, just like Charlie Siringo, the stove-up Texas cowboy. We read about him in a book."

Fargo smiled at them as one would a couple of mischievous children. "What those New York pulp writers don't tell is what it's really like bein' a cowboy. Charlie Siringo wasn't just stove up, his kidneys were shuttin' down on him from a steady diet of beans and bourbon. He looked sixty when he was thirty, his feet were so bad from wearin' boots even his corns had corns, and he had piles from sitting atop a horse all day long." Fargo sipped his coffee. He said, "That what you boys want?"

"What we want," Ferdie said, "is a taste of the cowboy life, not a career."

"And it should be a fun taste," Corny put in.

"We'll give you five hundred dollars," Ferdie said, "and money for expenses, whatever comes up."

Fargo couldn't help but look interested. He said, "You got that kind of money on you?"

Ferdie pulled a billfold from his pants pocket and counted out five hundred, dropping the bills on the table.

"Do we have a deal?" Ferdie asked.

Fargo said, "If you can pay me five hundred, you can probably afford seven-fifty."

Ferdie looked at his friend quizzically. Corny leaned over and whispered something in Ferdie's ear. Ferdie whispered something back. Corny shook his head. Ferdie looked exasperated, then counted out five fifties from the billfold.

"Seven-fifty," Ferdie said, a little snidely. "Care to count it?"

"I'll count it when there's a thousand on the table," Fargo said.

"A thousand?" Ferdie gasped.

"I would've settled for seven-fifty," Fargo said to Ferdie, "but then I decided that with such a bad attitude as you have, it's gonna cost you an extra two-fifty."

"That's a little high," Ferdie said.

"Heaven is higher," Fargo said, "and there's a good chance you'll be spendin' some time there with that right smart mouth of yours." Fargo rose from his chair and jammed his hat on his head. "My price is one thousand dollars. That's five hundred dollars per ass, both of which I think I'll be a-savin' from certain death."

He tossed fifty cents onto the table for his meal. His last fifty cents. There was seven hundred and fifty dollars there for the taking but, Fargo knew, money talked louder when a man was prepared to walk away from it.

Fargo went toward the door. He could hear the Easterners arguing in hushed tones. Corny said, "It's worth the extra money. He *did* save our lives, after all."

They argued back and forth for a moment.

"Tether your horse, Mr. Fargo," Ferdie finally said, plopping more bills on the pile. "One thousand dollars. And we'd better have lots and lots of fun."

Fargo turned and scooped up the money. Barring any unforeseen circumstances—like women and poker—Fargo could live on a thousand dollars for a high-on-the-hog month or two. Maybe even six months, if he lived clean.

"Just bought yourself a teacher, boys," Fargo said. He jammed the money into his pocket and sat down again.

"So," he said, "what would you guys like to do first?"

Ferdie leaned over and whispered again in Corny's ear. Corny nodded. Ferdie turned to Fargo and said, "We'd really like to rob a bank."

5

Fargo tossed the thousand dollars back onto the table as if the bills had leprosy.

"Rob a bank?" Fargo said. "Are you boys loco?"

"Ferdie and I thought robbing a bank might be fun," Corny said.

"You *are* serious," Fargo said, standing abruptly, knocking his chair backwards. "I don't know what's in that New York water you boys drink, but it's sure as hell affected your thinkin'. Robbing a bank's as good as kissin' your butts goodbye. Folks in San Angelo don't take too kindly to folks stealin' their life savings, and most of 'em carry guns. You guys won't live long enough to get on a wanted poster."

"We will if we plan properly," Ferdie said. "I've got it all worked out." He pulled a wrinkled piece of paper from his shirt pocket and spread it out on the table. Fargo rolled his eyes at the elaborate artwork, complete with arrows and measurements and a series of pictures of minutes ticking off a clock. Cartoon cowboys with masks over their faces aiming big guns at other cartoon people behind tellers' cages. Below the illustration was a lot of writing, most of it frenzied, with lots of crossed out words.

Fargo pushed the paper away. He said, "Given it some thought, have you?"

Ferdie tapped a forefinger on the paper, saying, "If my logistics are correct, we can take every dollar in the place and not have to hurt anybody. Here's how it works: we leave Corny here with the horses outside, then push through the doors, firing into the ceiling. Then we—"

Fargo held out his hand. "Just hold off there," he said.

"Were you boys thinkin' about any bank in particular, or one in Texas? You ever been inside one?"

"A bank is a bank," Ferdie said. "I imagine one is the same as the next."

"Not in San Angelo," Fargo said. "You won't make it, believe me."

"We agree, Mr. Fargo," Ferdie said. "Not without someone like yourself helping us."

Ferdie smiled, but there was no mirth in it. He'd made up his mind to rob a bank, and one way or another he would. And he would die, Fargo knew, either in the bank or at the hands of a posse later on. His friend, this amiable, innocent kid named Corny, would also die. These Eastern youth knew nothing about the true Texas.

They weren't bad kids, just a couple of trouble-making boys who were pointed in the wrong direction. Stupid as they were, they certainly didn't deserve to eat any bullets.

Robbing a bank. Fargo studied on it. There were plenty of banks in San Angelo. Surely he could find one banker who would be willing to take a bribe to indulge a couple of spoiled brats from back East who dreamed of guts and glory and conquering a harsh world called the American West. These boys had money to burn; certainly someone could be found to help them burn it.

"All right," Fargo said. "Let's suppose I can set up a bank robbery. Suppose we even get away with it. Then what?"

"Oh, we wouldn't keep the money," Corny said. "We'd send it back. Ferdie and I just want to see if we can pull it off, that's all."

Fargo ran his fingers through his hair. He said, "What's in it for me?"

"Another five hundred dollars if we're successful," Ferdie said. "In the meantime, I think it would behoove you to take our money." He was smiling, but his eyes were colder than Missouri winter. This was a young man used to getting what he wanted. Fargo wasn't sure if he liked him or not. Still, his money was as green as any man's.

Fargo looked Ferdie square in the eye and said, "Let me study on it."

"Fine," Ferdie said. "What happens next?"

"You boys got any lodgin'?" Fargo asked. "You stoppin' anywhere or what?"

"We just rolled into town," Ferdie said.

"A few hours ago," Corny added.

"Then here's what you do," Fargo said, looking at them all urgent-like. "You boys go get yourselves a couple of rooms at the Half Moon Hotel down the block."

"All right," Ferdie said. "We rent some rooms at a hotel. Then what?"

"Stay there until I come back to you—" Fargo said.

Ferdie whispered something at Corny. Corny whispered something back. Ferdie then said to Fargo, "All right, Mr. Fargo. We'll wait. But we're trusting you."

"That's good," Fargo said, taking their money again. He made his way to the door. "I'll see what I can do," he said. "Don't do anything till you hear from me."

6

"Mr. Fargo, do you know what you're asking?" Henry P. Twerk asked indignantly. He was a squat man with a bald spot the size of a silver dollar, wearing a suit that was several sizes too small and a black necktie that rode his several chins.

"I think I do," Fargo said, shifting uncomfortably in the wooden chair opposite Twerk's desk. "Can you help me or not?"

Henry P. Twerk wore the expression of a man who was being confronted by an escaped lunatic. And with good reason, Fargo mused.

Fargo, a total stranger, had wandered in off the street and offered the tubby bank president two hundred dollars to help him stage a mock robbery, just to satisfy the wild-west whims of a couple of rich Eastern kids. Was it any wonder Henry P. Twerk looked like he'd just smelled a sour horse turd?

"Let me get this straight," Twerk said. "Your friends aren't interested in the money, per se. They're only interested in the actual excitement of robbing a Texas bank."

"Well yes," Fargo said. "My idea, Mr. Twerk, was this: fill up a couple of money bags with metal washers or something, and hand them over. My friends won't know any different because they have no idea I've set this up. They'll think they're actually going to rob a real bank. And since I've already made them promise they'd return the stolen money—in this case metal washers—you'll be several hundred dollars richer, and no one will be any the wiser."

Henry P. Twerk didn't look wholly convinced. There was no good reason he should. What Fargo was asking was sheer madness.

Twerk leaned back in his chair and folded his hands across the wide expanse of girth. "This is a most unusual request, Mr. Fargo," Twerk said. "Asking permission to rob a bank, I can't say I've heard that one before. What possibly made you think I would ever agree, for any amount of money, to entertain such a harebrained notion?"

"I know it does indeed sound crazy, Mr. Twerk," Fargo said. "Especially since I'm a complete stranger and all."

"For starters, yes," Twerk agreed.

"I mean, it's not like you know me or anything," Fargo said. "Seeing how I just rolled into town a week ago. But may I say a few things in my defense?"

Twerk said, "It's a free country, Mr. Fargo." There was something about this man, Twerk thought, that inspired trust. Men who looked you straight in the eye, who laid their cards on the table and had no apparent axes to grind, were generally a safe bet. And Skye Fargo seemed like an honest man, as honest men went. Still, his request was so incredibly outlandish it almost defied any amount of dollars and cents logic the stout banker possessed.

"I've been around, Mr. Twerk," Fargo said. "I assumed you'd want some sort of references. I have friends and acquaintances from Kansas City to Seattle. The Pinkertons, the Texas Rangers, lawmen all over the West, and yes, even some folks in Washington will happily vouch for my character."

Twerk looked dubious. He said, "I don't doubt that, sir. A man in my position must be a shrewd judge of character, and you seem okay on the surface. But two hundred dollars hardly seems worth the goodwill and the tarnished image my bank will receive as a result of any robbery, bogus or otherwise. Surely you can understand this."

Fargo did. In fact, he'd anticipated it.

He said, "Of course you're right, Mr. Twerk. Thank you for your time."

He stood and jammed his hat on his head. He extended his hand to the portly banker, who took it and also stood.

"I'm sorry I cannot accommodate you, Mr. Fargo," Henry P. Twerk said. "However, there are several other banking establishments in town that might perhaps be more receptive to your idea."

"I'm sure there are," Fargo said. "And I'm also sure

they're well aware of the names Ferdinand Wallingford and Hiram Cornelius Fisk." He turned to leave, jangling his spurs for dramatic effect.

"Wallingford, did you say?" Twerk asked. "Of the Wallingford Maritime Company of New York?"

"The very one," Fargo said. "You've heard of him?"

"I'd hardly be in the banking business if I didn't, sir," Twerk said. "And Hiram Cornelius Fisk—I believe I'm familiar with his establishment as well. The Fisk Savings and Loan in New York?"

"Yep," Fargo said. "I've been keeping their wayward sons safe from harm. For a price of course, but they trust me implicitly."

"Do tell," Twerk said, interested now. His little beady black eyes lit up like burning lumps of coal.

Fargo moved in for the kill. He said, "It's my understanding that their fathers are looking to widely expand their holdings. That's one reason their sons are here, of course, to scout out new investment opportunities. This is private information of course, but I can't think of a better territory than Texas, or a better town than San Angelo. Or a better man to handle such transactions as your ownself."

"Well," Twerk said, a bit flustered now. He took a handkerchief and mopped his sweaty fat face. "This is a horse of a much different color, isn't it?"

"I guess so," Fargo said.

Henry P. Twerk opened a desk drawer and pulled out a bottle of whiskey and two glasses. He poured each of them a drink. Fargo sat and took the offered glass. From the aroma alone, Fargo could tell the whiskey was quality stuff, not rotgut.

"I'll have to make a few discreet inquiries, of course," Twerk said. "But I'm sure we can come to some sort of agreement."

"I'm sure we can, Mr. Twerk," Fargo said.

Twerk took a cigar from his vest pocket, offered it to Fargo.

"Cigar?" he asked.

"Don't mind if I do," Fargo said. He bit the end off and took a light from Twerk.

Fargo puffed contentedly. "I congratulate you for having such an open mind, Mr. Twerk."

"Having an open mind, Mr. Fargo," Twerk said, "is what made me the success I am today."

"And will make you two hundred dollars richer," Fargo said, raising his glass. "For a scant few minutes' work."

"As I say," Twerk said. "I'll have to make a few inquiries. Strictly routine of course, but I'll need a day or two."

"Can you make it just a day?" Fargo asked. "My friends are very eager to prove their manhood. Boys will be boys, you know."

"Perhaps I can," Twerk said. "Where are you stopping sir?"

"The Half Moon Hotel," Fargo said. He knew the Half Moon was as fancy a hotel as San Angelo had to offer.

"A fine establishment," Twerk said approvingly. "I'll be in touch tomorrow."

"The sooner the better," Fargo said.

"Of course," Twerk said, and clinked Fargo's glass with his own. "To your health, sir."

"And to yours," Fargo said. If only all of life was this easy, he mused.

"Either of you boys ever been laid?" Fargo asked.

They were strolling leisurely down the street. The setting sun was a giant, orange fireball in the west. Corny had never seen a sun so huge. It hardly looked like the smaller one that disappeared into the scummy Hudson River every evening back home in New York City.

Sex. Ferdinand I had instructed him on the basics one night after Bridget had decided their son needed to know the facts of life. "A man can't be too careful when it comes to getting the midnight drip," Wallingford I had told Ferdie Jr. "The urge gets too strong you're better off choking your chicken. You know—Mary Palmer and her five sisters."

When his son looked quizzically at him, Ferdie Senior jerked his fist up and down until the boy got the message. The elder Wallingford rolled his eyes in disgust and said, "If you aren't already doing it three times a day, you damn well should be."

Since that fateful day, Ferdie had done just that. Regardless, it failed to totally satisfy the deep carnal cravings for any woman not named Mary Palmer.

"Laid?" Corny asked Fargo.

"Yeah, laid," Fargo said. "She's got it, you want it, she says okay, then *you* get it."

"Oh, that," Corny said. "Sure, millions of times."

"Me, too," Ferdie put in.

"I didn't think so," Fargo said. "Hell, you come this far west to be cowboys, you got to at least sample our Texas hospitality. And there's a half dozen examples of it yonder."

He pointed to a gaudily painted, red clapboard house nestled between the telegraph office and Drake's Bakery.

"Pretty, pink, and plump, just right for plucking . . . for a price, of course."

Two horses were tied to a hitching post out front. Corny and Ferdie could hear piano music tinkling inside. A drunken cowpoke, stark naked, staggered out of the whorehouse, clutching a huge bottle of fizzy French wine. "I do sooooo love this place," he cried in alcoholic glee, then fell face down into the dusty street.

The place was called "Aunt Nellie's Pleasure Palace and Gambling Emporium," so proclaimed by a huge wooden banner that stretched halfway across the veranda. Below this was "Founded 1846."

"A satisfied customer," Fargo said, prodding the passed-out cowboy with the tip of his boot, "is the best advertisement."

Corny and Ferdie stood motionless, their faces chalky white. Fargo looked to them both, and said, "You comin', pardners?"

Ferdie looked at Corny. Corny's eyes were larger than doilies. His expression was one of stark terror and excited anticipation. Ferdie felt much the same reaction.

"It's a whorehouse," Ferdie said to his friend.

"The kind our daddies warned us about," Corny said.

"If my daddy warned me about it," Ferdie said, "then chances are he was speaking from experience."

"So how far has your apple fallen from his tree," Corny asked.

"Close enough to let me nail a Texas blonde tonight," Ferdie said.

"Me, I'll settle for any woman," Corny said. "Shall we?"

"Bet your ass we shall," Ferdie exclaimed. "Our fathers be damned."

Indeed, Corny had never been with a woman in the biblical sense—unless one included the time with Sally, the upstairs maid. Sally was a hot-blooded Irish gal from County Cork who was teaching Ferdie how to kiss and let him touch her breasts—in the broom closet, when his father found them and fired her immediately. Unfortunately, Corny had gotten no further with Sally.

Whatever had or hadn't happened in the past no longer mattered. Inside that house were real women, which meant that Mary Palmer could have the night off, and neither boy would have to hump his mattress tonight. They started to follow Fargo inside. Ferdie grabbed Corny's shoulder.

"We won't get the midnight drip, will we?"

"I don't know just what that is," Corny said, looking ready to explode with lust. "But let's hope it's something terrific."

A fat woman, her face covered with so much makeup Ferdie was sure she applied it with a cake decorator, greeted Fargo warmly. She was short and round, forty if she was a day, and her hair was a dizzying mess of dyed brown spitcurls. Melon-sized breasts fought at the constraints of a too-tight gingham dress, threatening to burst free and smother him at any given moment.

"Skye Fargo, as I live and breathe," the fat woman gushed happily, grabbing him and shoving his face between her massive boobs. This was, Ferdie decided, Aunt Nellie.

"Hello, Nellie," Fargo said through muffled gasps. "It's been a long time." Nellie's breasts were easily the seventh and eighth wonders of the world. He freed himself from her strong arms and motioned to his new friends.

"I'd like you to meet Misters Wallingford and Fisk," Fargo said. "They're new in town and lookin' for a good time."

Aunt Nellie eyeballed Fargo's friends. A couple of green kids who between them hadn't sowed a single wild oat. Nellie grinned—she loved new challenges.

"Well," Aunt Nellie said, scanning them up and down like a Fort Worth cattle buyer. "I do believe we can show them a good time and leave them with a few memories to take home."

"Had no doubt you could, Nellie," Fargo said. "I figure we ought to introduce them to your staff."

There were half a dozen whores lounging around the plushly decorated parlor. Some were pleasingly plump; others were tall and thin. They had one thing in common, however—they were all big-breasted and available.

Ferdie was strongly attracted to a pretty brunette who had high cheekbones and long black hair. She was sprawled lazily on a velvet couch, clad only in a frilly nightgown. The nails on her fingers and toes were painted bright red. She smiled at Ferdie, who found himself smiling back. There was a pleasant tingle in his loins.

"Don't think any introductions'll be necessary," Fargo said, motioning to Ferdie. "Looks like Mr. Wallingford's made his choice."

Aunt Nellie, who ran the finest house in West Texas, gently prodded Ferdie from behind. "Go sit next to her, sweetie," she said to Ferdie. "Louise don't bite. Got some Cherokee blood in her. She'll sling your ass all over the bed if you want her to."

Ferdie went and sat next to her on the couch, only a few feet away.

"Sit closer, honey," Louise said in a husky voice. "We won't get far with you sitting in the next county."

Ferdie moved closer. Louise draped her long, shapely legs across Ferdie's lap and wiggled her toes.

"Be a dear and rub my feet," Louise said.

Ferdie nervously took hold of Louise's feet. As feet went, they were quite nice. He held them in his hands like they were a pair of freshly caught trout, not knowing what to do next.

"Louise likes her feet rubbed to get her in the mood," Aunt Nellie explained. "Let's see about getting Mr. Fisk accommodated."

Just then, a short, rotund woman padded into the parlor, the kitchen door swinging shut behind her. She stood all of five feet tall. She was wearing a nightie that left little to the imagination, not that at man would necessarily want to imagine it.

The young lady—she looked no more than eighteen—was munching hungrily on a chicken leg. She had short, plump legs and breasts that could have doubled for cannonballs. They jiggled like two piglets wrestling in a potato sack.

"Lulubelle," Aunt Nellie said. "Got someone who wants to meet you."

"Do I pay her by the hour or by the pound?" Corny whispered to Fargo.

Aunt Nellie escorted Lulubelle over to Corny, whose eyes were riveted to her mammoth breasts. Lulubelle had flaming red hair and dumpling-like cheeks that folded into creases when she smiled.

"Say hello to Mr. Fisk, Lulubelle," Aunt Nellie said.

Lulubelle descended on Corny, and engulfed him in her massive arms. She gave him a long, passionate kiss, squeezing the breath out of him. Lulubelle wouldn't have been Corny's first choice, exactly—there was a blonde sitting at the piano he would have preferred—but his choice seemed to have been made for him. Lulubelle broke off the kiss and roughly grabbed Corny by the shoulder. She half-walked, half-dragged him up the stairs. Poor Corny looked like a man who was drowning in the sea of love.

"You and me is going to get us better acquainted," Lulubelle said, still munching on the chicken leg. A moment later, Louise took Ferdie's hand and similarly guided him up the stairs.

At the top of the staircase, Corny turned to his friend. He said, looking desperate, "Which dime novel was this one in?"

"None that I can remember," Ferdie said, watching Louise's behind as she made her way slinkily down the hall towards her room. "I think we have to write our own from here on in."

Lulubelle opened the door to her room and started to pull Corny inside. "That's what I was afraid of," Corny gulped.

Downstairs, Aunt Nellie said to Fargo, "Them gals are the two hottest spit-fires in San Angelo. Hope they leave enough of them boys to take home."

"Best not wear 'em out too much, Nellie," Fargo said. "They got something important to do tomorrow."

Aunt Nellie poked him and smiled, "Ain't gonna let your friends there have all the fun, are you?"

He most certainly was not. He surveyed the remaining

talent on display in Nellie's parlor and opted for a cute, thin, but ample-breasted dirty blonde. She didn't look as hard-edged as some of the other girls in Nellie's employ. The girl grinned nervously at Fargo.

Nellie, ever the observant businesswoman, motioned to her. The girl rose from the overstuffed armchair she'd been lounging in. She took Fargo by the hand and led him slowly up the stairs. Nellie called out behind him, "Let me know how she does, Mr. Skye. She just arrived this morning. You're her first."

"You got a name?" Fargo asked the girl as he eyed her up and down.

Her name was Emma Lansdale, from Nacogdoches. She was the daughter of a dirt farmer who married—some would say sold—her off at the age of fourteen to the town blacksmith, an unshaven, foul-smelling widower named Otto Fries. When she resisted his advances on their wedding night, he beat her. The marriage only lasted three days, mostly because Emma was sage enough to run away. Since then, over two years ago, she'd been working as a waitress in the cathouse circuit across Texas but only, she later pointed out, in the finest houses in Houston, Fort Worth, and now San Angelo.

Once inside the room, she started undressing slowly.

"Am I really your first . . . customer?" Fargo asked.

She nodded and said, "I guess you are."

"We don't have to do this if you're scared," Fargo said.

"You're my first here, not my first ever," she said with a smile. "How would you like a nice hot bath."

"Will you be there?" Fargo asked.

Emma giggled.

Five minutes later, in another room down the hall, Fargo was luxuriating in a claw-foot tub filled with lots of hot water and sweet-smelling suds. Emma, dressed down to her panties, was leaning over him, soaping his chest slowly. Fargo was highly aroused below the waist.

A fat black maid came in with another pail of hot water and poured it into the tub. Fargo fumbled, trying to cover his swollen manhood.

The black woman said to him, leaving, "Don't you worry,

41

chile'. Unless you got two of 'em, it's nothing I ain't seen before."

"Thank you, Octavia," Emma said, and went to work on Fargo, soaping his belly, moving slowly and lovingly south. She soaped up his stiff rod, her luscious melons hanging in his face, and said admiringly, "You sure got a real nice one, Skye."

How did one respond to a compliment like that? Instead, he started playing with her ample breasts. She tried to pull away, but Fargo pulled her back. Losing her balance, she plunged into the tub on top of him.

"Now don't that beat all," Fargo said, groping for her.

She wriggled free of his grasp and said, "We ain't gonna 'complish much in a bathtub. I reckon you're clean enough, tall man. Let's go back to my room and have some real fun."

"I'm right behind you," Fargo said, and hoisted himself out of the tub.

Emma handed him a nice soft towel and said, "Wrap that around your waist," she said. "I don't want the other girls seein' you. They may get ideas."

Back inside her room, Emma climbed onto the bed and, sitting on her knees, peeled off her soggy undergarments. Fargo's manhood was like a tent pole under the wet towel.

She had the most beautiful bosoms he'd ever seen: firm, perfectly rounded with plump nipples that cried for immediate attention. Her figure was a gift from the gods, flawlessly chiseled, with all the peaks and valleys a healthy, red-blooded man could hope for. In the dim lantern light of the room, Fargo marveled at the sight of her.

"If you wanna make love to me, darlin'," Emma said, "then you're a-gonna have to meet me at least halfway."

Fargo let the towel drop from his waist. He went to her, climbing onto the bed. Emma blew out the flame in the lantern and laid on her back. Fargo slid on top of her, pressing his chest against her breasts. He could feel her taut nipples rubbing against him as she took him in her arms and held him tightly.

He kissed her passionately, sliding his tongue into her mouth. She took it eagerly, kissing him back with just as much gusto. She wrapped her legs around his, feeling him throb against her belly, and breathed in his ear, "Do any old thing you want, tall man."

What Fargo did was sample her delectable left nipple, sucking and licking it, biting it gently, which brought a moan of pleasure from Emma. She ran her fingers through his damp hair and guided him to her other nipple, where he started all over again. After several more moans, she rolled Fargo onto his back and said, "Let me give you something sweet, lover."

Emma gently clenched the shaft of his pulsing manhood and took it deeply into her mouth. She lovingly ran her tongue along the underside. Fargo gripped the sheets on the side of the bed, groaning in ecstasy as Emma continued her eager assault on his stiffness.

Then she was back in his arms, which were quickly all over her, running up and down the length of her body and giving her tight rear a squeeze every now and then.

Emma whispered, "I want you on top of me again, tall man."

Fargo held her firmly and rolled on top of her. Emma eagerly spread her legs, and Fargo entered her slowly. Emma wrapped her legs around his, forcing his firm hotness more deeply into her tight, wet glove. Fargo began to thrust rhythmically, Emma writhing under him, running the soles of her feet up and down his legs. She raised her butt up and down in perfect timing to his thrusts.

Emma nibbled on his ear bucking up and down as the intensity of their lovemaking rose to a feverish pitch. Fargo knew he would not be able to hold back much longer, though he tried to prolong the pleasure. Fate had other plans, however, and soon he felt the familiar, pleasant tingling deep within his groin. His thrusting grew stronger, and seconds later he exploded inside of her. Emma cried out in ecstasy, dragging her red-painted fingernails across his strong, taut back, drawing a few drops of blood. They held each other as tightly as a man and a woman could, becoming one as their bodies stiffened in climax.

Fargo felt sorry for anyone who wasn't him tonight.

When the flames of their love ebbed, Fargo kissed her affectionately and said softly, "I think I could learn to love you."

"I'll be here whenever you want me, tall man," Emma said.

They started kissing once more, with even greater passion than before, and were well on their way to making love again when there came a sharp knock on the door, and Nellie's voice calling out, "Time!"

"Shit!" they cried in perfect unison.

7

At approximately the same time that Fargo and his new friends were sampling the tasty goods at Aunt Nellie's, a group of men huddled around a campfire some six miles outside San Angelo.

Deke Lonegan took a sip of the bitter, scalding-hot coffee and said to Al Bridge, "Tell me again."

Al Bridge spit into the campfire and said, "It's pure velvet, Deke. All they got are a couple of kid tellers—ain't neither one of 'em barely old enough to shave—and a bucket-butt of a bank manager."

Deke Lonegan nodded, seemingly satisfied. Al Bridge poured himself a cup of coffee, all the while watching his boss think, digesting the facts. "How many total in the bank?" Lonegan wanted to know.

Bridge said, "Three."

"And no guns on any of 'em?" Lonegan asked.

"Nope," Bridge said. "And the closest law is two streets away."

The boss seemed to like this. Deke Lonegan tossed the dregs of his coffee into the fire and stood. "Then that clinches it," he said. "We take the bank tomorrow." He'd already checked out San Angelo when they'd first ridden into town, and had deemed it suitable for a little plundering.

Lonegan gazed across the campfire at his hand-picked band of outlaws, a motley collection of hardcases he'd culled from several dozen murder raids. All of his men had one thing in common: there were wanted posters and necktie parties awaiting them in small towns and cities across the West.

Ned Thornton was pouring a slug of whiskey into his

coffee. Deke Lonegan looked at the gaunt, hawk-faced out-law with some concern. Thornton was a cold-blooded killer who'd blast his own grandmother into the great beyond for a boodle of bank money. Lonegan had found him in a shithole of a saloon outside Oklahoma City. Thornton had just drilled an uppity bartender with three shots to the chest for spilling whiskey on him.

Lonegan moved his gaze around the fire. His men were four of the scurviest lowlifes to ever draw a breath. Beside Thornton and Al Bridge, there was Pee Wee Parker, a rat-faced hothead from Arkansas whose skills lay in killing first and asking questions later. He'd joined up with Lonegan back in Missouri, where they'd ambushed a stagecoach, kill-ing three women and two children, the youngest only eight years old. For a moment, Lonegan's gaze stopped at Pee Wee who was across the campfire skinning a couple of rab-bits he'd shot a few hours before, squeezing the blood out of the carcasses like water from a sponge. Some drops landed on his hand. Pee Wee licked them off. Fried rabbit and rotgut, a dining favorite for the Lonegan gang.

Flat-Eye Quan sat by the fire and rocked back and forth pensively, chewing on one of his fingers. Flat-Eye was the product of a Chinese railroad worker and a consumptive Mexican whore. He had a pear-shaped head and not a hair on his body. He was mostly an idiot and grinned all the time. More often than not, spittle oozed out of the left corner of his mouth. Flat-Eye Quan pleasured himself with hurting living things, be they man or beast. When he wasn't chewing his finger, he preferred to carve up one of his arms or hands, just to see the sight of blood flowing.

"Gonna have us some cooked rabbit, Flat-Eye," Lonegan said, eyeing the crazy bastard. "Ain't no need to et your ownself."

Flat-Eye, without the slightest sign of any intelligence flickering in his eyes, looked at Lonegan. He then looked at his raw, bloody finger and wished he'd gotten the job of squeezing the blood from the dead rabbits instead of Pee Wee. Lonegan never let him skin their dinner, as Flat-Eye tended to slash supper into inedible shreds.

No doubt about it, Deke Lonegan was more than pleased with his happy band of killers. He figured they'd head west to Arizona Territory after tomorrow's robbery; his boys would happily ride through the gates of Hell with their beloved Deke Lonegan, who had a first-rate reputation within the outlaw community. He was a man who made things happen and almost always kept his people alive so they could enjoy the fruits of their endeavors.

Pee Wee put the filleted rabbits on the fire and cooked them with great care. Ned Thornton took a swig of rotgut from the bottle. Lonegan watched him closely. Thornton was a trouble-making ne'er do well, or at least had that potential.

"Don't see why we got to plan anything," Ned Thornton said. "Was it me, I'd go in with guns blazing 'n kill whoever's there. Take the money and screw ever'thing else."

Bridge regarded his boss. He and Deke Lonegan had been together for damn near ten years and it had been made very clear that the boss didn't buck any disrespect. Lonegan listened to Thornton's suggestion, as though actually taking it seriously and shot a gob of spit into the fire. There was a foul-smelling hiss as it hit the flame. Lonegan gave Thornton a look that could curdle fresh milk.

"You got a problem with my plan?" Lonegan asked Thornton.

Thornton spit back into the fire, letting loose a stream longer than Lonegan's had been. "Ain't said I got any problem," Thornton grunted. "Just said we could make it easier by blastin' ever'thing in sight."

Lonegan grinned, having himself a private joke. His eyes flashed a menacing stare. "If you was any dumber, boy, you'd already be dead."

Thornton bristled at Lonegan's comment and went for his Colt. Before he even touched gunmetal, two shots rang out and kicked up a big puff of dust at Thornton's feet. Lonegan had his gun aimed at Thornton's groin; a fatal gut-shot was two inches higher. Thornton, pure hatred blazing in his eyes, stared back at Lonegan. Thornton was a man who knew he was close to being beat, and hated the idea.

"I think you're full of shit," Thornton said. "Was I running this bunch, things would be done different."

Thornton had the gang's attention. They were watching him closely. Who could tell—before the night was out—that Ned Thornton just might be running the show.

Lonegan holstered his pistol. Thornton seized the opportunity and went for his Colt. Lonegan cleared leather before Thornton even came close. One shot rang out. Pee Wee, Flat-Eye, and Al Bridge rolled backwards away from the fire. Lonegan's shot made Thornton's kneecap explode.

Thornton howled in agony, clutching his left leg. Lonegan stood up and turned to Flat-Eye, "May I kindly borry your knife?"

He extended his hand to the odd-looking Flat-Eye, who handed his knife over to Lonegan without question. Thornton continued howling in pain. Lonegan, clutching the knife in his fist, walked slowly around the fire to where Thornton was moaning and clutching his wounded leg.

"Do we still have a problem, Mr. Thornton?" Lonegan asked him.

Blood gushed from Thornton's shattered leg. He tried hard to look straight into Lonegan's coal black eyes. It wasn't easy.

"You go to hell," Thornton said between gritted teeth.

"After you, Mr. Thornton," Deke Lonegan said.

Pee Wee, Al Bridge, and Flat-Eye only saw the glint of metal in the dim firelight as Lonegan arced the knife through the cool night air. Half a second later, Ned Thornton howled in pain a second time. Deke Lonegan was holding a freshly severed ear in the palm of his hand.

Thornton's hand went up to the left side of his head as he tried to contain the blood that now seeped between his fingers. He started whimpering as the shock of losing an important part of his anatomy set in. Lonegan casually tossed the severed ear over his shoulder.

"From the very day I watched you shoot that bartender in Oklahoma Territory, I knew you would be trouble," Lonegan said, standing over him. "Knew it come to this someday."

Lonegan pulled out his gun and aimed it straight at Thornton's head.

"Don't do this, Deke," Thornton pleaded. "I didn't mean no disrespect."

"Oh, but you did," Lonegan said. "Otherwise, you wouldn't have no bullet in your leg." He shook his head sadly. "I've killed dozens of your type, son. One won't make no never mind."

He cocked his pistol, still aimed at Thornton's head.

"Trouble with you young folks," Lonegan said, "you ain't go no respect for your betters."

"I'm sorry, Deke," Thornton said breathlessly, his color growing paler in the dim firelight. "Have mercy on my soul."

"Sorry, Ned," Lonegan said. "You made me look bad, and I can't be havin' that. When a man makes me look bad, my milk of human kindness goes dry at the tit."

Lonegan fired one shot into Thornton's brain. The top of Thornton's head exploded, brains and blood splattering all over the gang. Thornton's body twitched a few times and then went still.

Lonegan twirled his pistol and holstered it in one quick motion. "Anyone else got somethin' to add?"

Nobody did.

"How do you like it, honey?" Lulubelle asked Corny, sounding a trifle bored. Concetta, their Mexican cook, had prepared a tasty baked ham for dinner, and there was plenty left. Lulubelle's mind was on the ham and not this nervous looking, skinny Yankee boy who undoubtedly had had sex only once or twice—most likely with himself.

"Like it?" Corny responded. He was standing against the bedroom door, watching in awe as Lulubelle flopped down onto the bed and spread her considerable girth over half of it. She rolled over onto her belly; Corny was reminded of a beached whale he'd seen once at Coney Island.

Lulubelle's formidable breasts heaved in exasperation.

"How do you want to do it, sugar?" Lulubelle asked. "On top or on the bottom?"

Corny wanted Ferdie's girl, but Ferdie already had her. He said, somewhat confused, "Bottom of what?"

Lulubelle sighed. The dinner ham was drying out by the moment. "Some men like to climb atop me and diddle with my titties or whatever," she said. "Others like it when I get atop them."

Corny wasn't about to let this woman, who seemed five feet in both directions, get on top of him at any cost. Still, doing it was doing it, and nobody said this had to be the most pleasant experience of his life—he just didn't want to be a virgin anymore. It suddenly dawned on him that he was supposed to be in control here, he was the pay*er* and Lulubelle was the pay*ee.* Her formidable girth and scowling countenance, however, indicated otherwise.

Corny attempted to seize control of the situation. He said, "If it's all right, I think I'd prefer getting on top. But only if it's all right with you." He started to sweat, realizing that he was just about to actually do it.

"Whatever," Lulubelle said, holding her arms out to him.

He went unsteadily to the bed, his heart pounding. Lulubelle laughed, "You a-gonna shed your britches, boy, or do you want to dry-hump all night long?"

Before he could even respond, Lulubelle, with an impatient grunt, leaped up, grabbed Corny by the neck and flung him down onto the bed. She yanked his boots off and dropped them to the floor. She started pulling off his britches, struggling mightily. She said, "You want to lift your butt up for a second, sugar?"

Corny complied, and instantly his pants were off. In true cowboy style, he wore nothing underneath. He was surprised to see that his manhood was standing tall and proud. Lulubelle was on him like a flash, crawling onto him on all fours. Her pendulous breasts loomed like twin hot air balloons over him. She squatted over his groin and grabbed his pecker. Corny gasped; it felt good when a hand other than his touched his manhood.

"It's okay to play with my titties if you're a mind to," Lulubelle said. "Ain't no extra charge."

Corny gingerly reached up and placed his hands on Lulubelle's breasts like they were two hot cakes right out of the oven. Lulubelle guided Corny's swollen member into her warm, wet honeypot. Corny gasped breathlessly once more, his eyeballs rolling around the sockets like two marbles in a punch bowl.

"You're in, honey, relax now," Lulubelle said.

I'm really doing it, Corny thought dimly. Then something pleasant tingled deep inside him and his bottom half seemed to explode. Much too soon, he thought, but then again, he never expected his first time to actually be fun, more of a necessity.

No sooner had Corny climaxed when Lulubelle climbed off him. She tossed his pants into his face, then did the same with his boots and socks. The heel of his left boot bounced off his forehead.

"Time to go, honey," Lulubelle said, and sat down at the vanity table in the corner of the room to repaint her chubby face.

Corny did as he was told. He scrambled into his blue jeans and pulled his boots on over his bare feet. He looked at his socks and, shrugging, stuffed them in his pocket. He awkwardly made his way to the bedroom door. Lulubelle said, "It's considered polite to financially compensate a young lady who's just shared her favors with you."

Corny figured out all by himself that she was asking for a tip. All things considered, it hardly seemed worth it, but he reached into his pocket and pulled out his bankroll. It seemed smaller than it had before. He pulled off a bill and handed it to her. He didn't see the denomination, and didn't care. Suddenly, he was as eager to get out of there as Lulubelle was to see him go.

"Thanks, sugar," Lulubelle said, stuffing the bill between her huge breasts. "You take care now, and don't let the door hit you where the Good Lord split you." She turned back to the mirror and her war paint.

On his way downstairs, Corny examined his bankroll. It was definitely smaller than it should have been.

Upstairs, Lulubelle took the three hundred dollars she'd deftly filched from the boy's pocket when she'd pulled his pants off. She tucked the bills into her money belt. She'd have to kick half of it back to Nellie, but what the hell.

8

Louise was bouncing up and down on Ferdie's stiff totem pole, her long, shiny black hair brushing his face.

Ferdie reached up and grabbed her luscious breasts, squeezing the nipples between his fingers. This seemed to excite her even more. She shuddered in ecstasy, or so it seemed to him.

Once they were alone in her room, she had offered Ferdie what she called her "five for ten." It was an offer he could not refuse: five different sex positions for ten dollars each. Louise had already exhausted three positions, exhausting Ferdie as well, and was embarking on the fourth. The first three were fairly standard: man on top, woman on top, and man and woman doing it sideways. Ferdie couldn't wait to see what number four was. He'd already climaxed once and, after a brief five-minute respite, was back at it.

He didn't have long to wait. Louise slid off of him and got onto her hands and knees, sticking her shapely butt in his face.

"Ever done it doggie-like?" Louise asked huskily.

"I may have, I'm not sure," Ferdie said. "What exactly do I have to do?"

"Ever see two mongrels doing it in the street?"

In fact, he had. In the middle of Gramercy Park, to be exact, when he was walking to church with his parents. He was nine, maybe ten at the time. Bridget had tried to shield him from the sight of the two dogs lustily humping in the noonday sun for one and all to see, but Ferdie had watched in lurid fascination.

"Yes," he said.

"On your knees, love," she said.

Ferdie kneeled behind her, his pecker throbbing. Louise waited a few moments, then realized he was unsure what to do next.

She said, "Take yourself in your hand, stick it in me, and let's get along little doggie."

Ferdie prodded her with the tip of his cock, and said, "You mean like this?"

"A little lower, honey, a little lower," she said.

Ferdie continued poking at her, and said in deeper voice, "You mean like this?"

Louise, the consummate professional, grabbed Ferdie's pulsing shaft and slid it into her. She said, "Grab my hips, lover, and hold on."

Ferdie did, and Louise started bucking, slamming her buttocks into him and grinding it in circles. Sweat dripped down Ferdie's face. He wondered if those dogs in the park had had this much fun.

"Pump me, honey, pump me," she said.

Ferdie didn't think they could actually get any closer, but he got into the rhythm of the moment and slammed his hips at her, allowing his swollen manhood to penetrate her deeper than he could have dreamed humanly possible.

Three more thrusts of her butt, and Ferdie exploded. This one was even better than the first. Just for the hell of it, Louise looked back at him and said, "Now howl like a cur, stud."

Ferdie did. A hoarse cry ripped from his throat. He didn't know why she'd told him to do it, and didn't particularly care. Nothing had ever felt so good.

Spent, he collapsed on the bed and curled into a ball, wanting to go straight to sleep.

Louise grinned. "You still got one more position coming, honey."

"Can I save it for a rainy day?" Ferdie asked.

"This is West Texas, honey, it only rains maybe three days a year."

"I'll wait," Ferdie said, and started snoring.

Louise slowly descended the stairs, looking quite beautiful. Down in the parlor, Fargo was sipping port wine with Aunt Nellie, and Corny was twirling his hat impatiently. It was just like Ferdie to have all the fun. They'd been waiting damn near an hour.

Fargo looked over at Louise coming down the stairs alone. "Sweet Jesus, she done ate him alive," he said.

Louise giggled. "Not hardly," she said. "He's sleeping like a baby."

"You best take your new friends home for the night, Fargo," Aunt Nellie said. "Tuck 'em into a bed that don't charge by the hour."

"Good advice, Nellie," Fargo said. He finished his wine and rose, saying to Corny, "Let's go get your partner."

"You service him pretty good, Louise?" Aunt Nellie asked, already knowing the answer. Louise was her best.

"Yes'm," Louise said, and disappeared into the kitchen.

Corny followed Fargo up the stairs to retrieve his friend. Ferdie always seemed to do better with women, and it sort of made Corny mad. Ferdie was always getting kissed first when they went out on dates together, always managed to touch some hidden, mysterious parts of girls while he, Corny, always got slapped for his efforts.

Fargo sensed Corny's muffled anger. At the top of the stairs, he said, "Don't fret boy, just 'cause your friend did better than you in the whore department. We can come back tomorrow and you can have some time with Louise if you're of a mind to."

"Maybe I will," Corny said, liking the idea.

"Now let's get your friend and put him to bed," Fargo said. "You, too. We got us a bank to rob tomorrow."

9

"Ladies and gentlemen," Ferdie said from behind a red bandana, "this here is a robbery."

The truth be told, the bank was empty. Henry P. Twerk had arranged with Fargo to open a half hour earlier than usual for this very purpose. The stout banker was alone.

Henry P. Twerk tried to look scared, but his heart wasn't in it. These two New York rich boys, even with bandanas covering their faces and sporting the most expensive fashions from Colt, hardly looked capable of robbing a piggy bank, much less a real one.

Twerk had even pressed his fat wife into the service, playing a small role in their bizarre scenario. On cue, twirling her parasol, a fat vision dressed in white came strolling through the door to the bank. Her husband winked at her, and she screamed in mock horror at the sight of the armed bandits.

Fargo rolled his eyes, sighing under his bandana. Let's not overdo it, he thought, watching the fat lady squeal. Still, she was convincing enough so that Ferdie and Corny stared at each other, unsure of what to do next. Neither wanted to shoot her, not that it would have mattered. Fargo had replaced the bullets in their pistols with powder blanks in the middle of the night while they slept—just in case one of them got carried away in the excitement.

They looked to Fargo for guidance. He shook his head and said, "Was it me, I'd ask the lady to stop screaming."

Ferdie turned to Mrs. Twerk. He said, "Ma'am, please stop screaming." He turned back to Fargo.

Fargo said, "Tell her if she doesn't stop, you'll be forced to take serious measures."

Corny considered this advice, then piped up, "If you

don't stop screaming, ma'am, we'll be forced to measure you seriously."

Fargo said, "Perfect, kid."

Having made her contribution to her husband's little playlet, Mrs. Twerk voluntarily went and sat in a wooden chair in the corner. Later that morning, she was to have her friends from the San Angelo Baptist Ladies League over for tea.

"What do you want?" Twerk asked, his arms aimed at the sky. "Money?"

"Money would be nice," Ferdie agreed. He hadn't figured on this being so easy.

Twerk, with Ferdie trailing him, went to the safe. They looked at it, then looked at each other. Corny asked, "What do we do now, Ferdie?"

Ferdie thought about it for a minute, then said to Henry P. Twerk, "I don't suppose you'd want to give me the combination?"

Twerk looked at Fargo. Fargo shook his head.

"I'm afraid I can't, son." Twerk said. "Sorry."

Ferdie drew his pistol and fired at the ceiling. Corny pulled out his gun and did the same. Wood splintered from the ceiling. Ferdie cried, "Give me the combination or . . . or—"

"Or you'll blow his butt off," Corny offered.

"Or I'll blow your butt off!" Ferdie cried.

Twerk said indignantly. "You stop that now, both of you. I won't have shooting in this establishment."

"Firearms ain't Christian, gentlemen," Mrs. Twerk said.

Twerk went to the safe and spun the dial this way and that, then swung it open. Ferdie tried peering into the open safe, but Twerk blocked his view.

"Do you mind?" Twerk said officiously. "This is private."

"Sorry," Ferdie said, backing away. He knocked over a tray of pennies and nickels sitting on the edge of a table behind the teller's cage. They splattered all over the floor with a melodious tinkling. Twerk turned and angrily muttered something under his breath. Mrs. Twerk barely suppressed a titter of amusement. Ferdie put his gun on the table and knelt to collect the scattered coins from the floor.

Corny got down on all fours and helped him scoop up the coins. Twerk pulled two sacks of washers out of the safe and slammed the door shut. He said, looking at the spilled money with exasperation, "Here's your money. Kindly take it and go."

Fargo shook his head. There had to be an easier way to make a living.

Deke Lonegan, flanked on either side by Al Bridge and Pee Wee Parker, rode leisurely down Main Street. As was custom, Flat-Eye Quan trailed behind. Their target loomed up toward the end of the block. They were a man short, according to the plan, but Lonegan wasn't worried.

They stepped up their pace, but not enough to attract attention. It was business as usual in San Angelo; the streets were busy but not overflowing.

"You know the routine," Lonegan said.

Al Bridge nodded. They had been down this route many times before.

They approached the bank and dismounted. Flat-Eye took their horses' reins and waited stoically behind. Flat-Eye wasn't the sharpest tool in the shed to be sure, but he did what he was told and was ready to kill anyone, anytime, for any reason. Good men like that were hard to find.

Deke Lonegan strode across the wooden sidewalk to the bank entrance. Al Bridge was backing him up, and Pee Wee Parker was right behind him. The little prick was proving to be pretty handy taking a bank, judging from their last three robberies in Arkansas Territory. Lonegan took a deep breath of the cool morning air. It was a beautiful, cloudless morning and he was feeling fine. He had no hangover and Ned Thornton was but a memory. Life was good. This robbery was going to be simpler than stealing a fresh-baked apple pie off a windowsill.

Deke Lonegan knocked some mud off his boots and tied the bandana over his mouth and nose. Bridge and Pee Wee did likewise.

Lonegan was smiling, despite his efforts not to. Stealing just made him plum happy.

The portly banker handed Corny the bogus bags. Ferdie was still picking up coins, even crawling into a corner to retrieve one that had fallen down a rathole. "Never mind, never mind. Just take the bags and go. I've got a bank to run," Twerk said hotly.

His gun forgotten, Ferdie carried the bags over to his friend and handed him one. Corny holstered his pistol and took the bag. They started to open the bags to examine their ill-gotten gains.

Fargo stopped them. "A good bank robber never counts his take until he's safely away from the place he just robbed."

Fargo figured that when Ferdie and Corny discovered the washers they'd be quite disappointed. He'd explain to them that robbing a bank is serious business, give them the whole speech about crime and punishment and young men's fantasies. Maybe then they'd go home to New York and Fargo could get back to his life.

Fargo motioned for his two young comrades to make tracks. The stout, pink-cheeked banker's wife was now knitting a shawl as she sat waiting for them to finish their business, looking quite unconcerned.

Fargo went for the door, but before he could even grab the knob, the door flew open and slammed him flat on the nose. Fargo felt something crunch, then fell hard on his ass, totally dazed. Everything that followed seemed like a dream, and a bad one at that. Fargo watched in a foggy haze.

Deke Lonegan wasn't quite prepared for what awaited him and his boys once they were inside the bank.

Damned if some young dudes, Sears-Roebuck tinhorns from the looks of them, weren't robbing the bank their ownselves. Both were holding white burlap sacks full of money.

For a brief moment, there was total silence in the place. Corny and Ferdie gawked at the three men who had just burst in, pistols drawn. The men were dirty and unshaven, wearing beat-up boots and crumpled hats, five layers of gritty prairie dust and alkali covering their mean faces. These men were the genuine article, dime-novel desperadoes right off the pages of *Great Western Yarns*.

Fargo was on the floor, blood gushing from his crushed nose, not quite comprehending what was going on.

Twerk looked at the new additions to Mr. Fargo's robbery party. Fargo had told him there'd be only three, himself and the two greenhorns from back East. Something wasn't quite right here.

Mrs. Twerk had stopped knitting and was watching now, the needles frozen in mid-stitch.

"I may be wrong, Deke," Pee Wee Parker said, "but I do believe we got beat to the draw."

Lonegan back-handed Pee Wee across the face. "Why don't you tell 'em where I was born, too."

"In all my days, I never had to wait on line to rob a bank," Al Bridge added.

Twerk looked over at Fargo. Something was definitely wrong.

"Who are you?" Deke Lonegan snarled at Corny and Ferdie through his filthy red bandana. "And just what the hell do you think y'all are doing?"

"We're robbing this bank," Ferdie said.

"I'll be dunked in pigshit if I don't believe this," Lonegan said.

Fargo's head cleared long enough for him to fathom that fate had just dealt him a wild card. As a gambling man, he crazily tried to figure the odds of one small bank being held up by two gangs at the same time. It didn't seem possible, but it appeared to be happening nonetheless. One of the men had called the other Deke. That could only mean it was Deke Lonegan, scourge of Texas. Bank robber, cattle rustler, and murderer—plain bad news.

Fargo figured he could draw his Colt and maybe take down Lonegan before his buddies force-fed Fargo a good half-pound of lead. On the other hand, making a play could turn into a massacre.

"Would somebody be kind enough to tell me just what the hell is going on here?" Twerk said hotly, then to Fargo, "You said there'd only be—"

"We're robbin' your goddamn bank is what we're doing, fatty," Lonegan snarled.

"Indeed," Twerk grunted. He turned to Fargo, who looked as surprised as everyone else.

Twerk said to Fargo, "Is this a part of the scenario you failed to tell me about?"

"Wish it was," Fargo said. "I'd advise you to take these men seriously, Mr. Twerk."

Lonegan saw that the vault was still open. Bags of money were nestled snugly inside, just there for the taking.

"He's right," Lonegan said.

"You mean you men are *real* bank robbers?" Twerk asked incredulously.

Ferdie thought, what does that make us? He had the sense to keep his mouth shut, though. Everything had seemed just a little too easy up until now, what with the banker showing no fear—that fat lady, too, for that matter.

"I do believe they're real, Mr. Twerk," Fargo said.

"Damn right we're real," Deke Lonegan said. "Give him the sack, kid."

Not wanting to displease Deke a second time, Pee Wee tossed the empty burlap sack at the banker's feet.

"Pick it up and fill it with money," Lonegan snapped. "And shake your fat ass."

"What a fool I was, to trust you," Twerk said to Fargo. "You set me up for this, didn't you? Set up a fake robbery so you could pull off a real one."

Twerk kicked up the burlap sack and tossed it back over to Deke Lonegan. "I'm sorry, boys, but the game is over. Your antics are no longer appreciated in this establishment." Twerk spotted Ferdie's gun on the counter, and grabbed it. He pointed it at Lonegan and said, "Now you all get the hell out of my bank."

Deke Lonegan suddenly felt tired and impatient. He hated unexpected problems during a robbery, and the only solution was to make that problem go away.

"So says you," Lonegan snarled, and squeezed off two shots from his pistol. Two red holes appeared in Twerk's forehead like magic, half an inch apart.

Ferdie and Corny's jaws dropped simultaneously. The portly banker stumbled backwards from the impact of the shots, but still stood. He looked surprised, blinking his eyes a couple of times. Fargo knew that the man was already dead but his legs had yet to receive the message.

Twerk wobbled for half a second like a drunk trying to keep his balance, then pitched forward and crashed to the floor, blood spurting. His head made a sickening splat against the wooden floor.

"Eeep." The sound gurgled up deep from Corny's throat. The fat lady jumped up from the chair, dropping her knitting, and screamed at an ear-shattering pitch. Ferdie wanted to scream as well, but a moment later, was glad he didn't.

Lonegan wheeled in his tracks and pumped two shots into the chubby woman. These weren't quite as clean. Ferdie watched in gut-churning horror as a ragged, bloody chunk of her face exploded and decorated the freshly painted white bank wall. She dropped to the floor like a sack of brass doorknobs.

"Shit," Fargo muttered.

"I think I'm going to throw up," Corny murmured to no one in particular. For his part, Ferdie wasn't as lucky. A stream of hot fluid cascaded down his leg and puddled in his left boot. Some of it missed and pooled on the floor.

Lonegan turned the gun on Corny and Ferdie. He said, "You boys don't mind iffen we rob this bank instead of y'all, do you?"

"I won't hold a grudge," Corny said, his voice sounding far away. "Will you, Ferdie?"

Ferdie shook his head furiously. "N-no."

The gunman looked down at the dark puddle forming at the young man's feet, and it wasn't from a leaky canteen. He grinned.

"Ought to try and control your vitals, boy," Lonegan said to him, the barrel of his gun still trained at the kid's chest. "Man oughtn't to piss his pants if he can help it."

Ferdie said, "I'll try to remember that."

Al Bridge set about picking up the sack and going to the safe. He started tossing bags of money into it. Lonegan had really made a bloody mess out of this one. They'd have to tear ass for Mexico.

Deke Lonegan kicked Pee Wee Parker in the butt and growled, "Help the man." Pee Wee did as he was told, grabbing bags of cash and shoving them into the sack.

Deke Lonegan then turned his attention from the two tinhorns and aimed his gun at Fargo.

"Skye Fargo, ain't you?" Lonegan asked, looking him up and down.

Fargo wiped the blood from his nose on his sleeve. He said, "Name's Parsons," Fargo said. "Ed Parsons."

"Okay," Lonegan said. "Whatever you say. But you're still Skye Fargo. I've heered about you."

"You got me mistaken for someone else," Fargo said. He'd never felt so damned humiliated in his entire life.

Lonegan sighed and then pressed the barrel of his pistol into Corny's ear. Corny felt a cold sweat pop out on his brow.

"Is that man's name Skye Fargo?" Lonegan asked him. "Tell the truth, boy. Confession is good for the soul."

Corny swallowed hard. In an unsteady voice he said, "I only know him as Ed Parsons."

Lonegan cocked his pistol. Corny squeezed his eyes shut, preparing himself for the worst. Fargo's heart skipped a beat. He'd encouraged and profited from the whims of these two Yankee boys, and now they were going to pay with their lives.

Al Bridge piped up, "We're all set here. Let's make tracks."

Lonegan turned his attention to Ferdie, pointing his gun at him. "Your friend tellin' me the truth, brother?"

"I . . . I've never . . . known him to lie, sir," Ferdie responded.

Fargo felt a brief tinge of pride. The boys may have been tinhorns, but there were definitely some guts there as well.

"We best be on our way," Al Bridge said. Pee Wee was clutching the sack full of money like a skinny, grubby Santa Claus. "No need for any more killing, neither. We got what we came for."

Lonegan's eyes narrowed into hostile little slits. He knew the law in Texas. Two killings would get you a hanging. Or a lynching. With a hanging, it was over with in a second. A lynching took longer and hurt worse. Deke Lonegan had felt the burn of tar and feathers up in Missouri when he was fifteen years old for beating the reverend's daughter with her own Bible until she was bleeding like Christ on the cross. That's what the little bitch got for holding back.

Crossing the street from the cafe, Deputy Marshal Tom Cash heard the shots ringing out from inside the bank. Cash was on his way to Drake's bakery across the street for some strawberry tarts that his Martha liked so much.

Frightened townspeople started scrambling for cover, women screamed and grabbed their runny-nosed children to the safety of the closest shop. Bank robberies had been few and far between since San Angelo became a lawful town.

Cash spun on the heels of his boots, pulling his pearl-handled Colt from his holster and taking three rapid steps in the direction of the bank. There were seven horses tied to the hitching post; Cash thought for a moment that seven men to rob one small bank was a bit extreme.

Flat-Eye Quan stepped out from behind a wooden post, his gun drawn, and squeezed off two shots at Cash. To his credit, Cash managed to fire once before Flat-Eye's bullets took him in the heart and left lung. He sank to his knees and pitched forward into the muddy street.

Flat-Eye heard some man shout, "They done shot Tom Cash!" Flat-Eye scrambled back to the bank and ducked his head inside.

"We go now," he gasped. "I shoot white man with tin star."

"That's it, Deke," Al Bridge said. "We got it all, let's make tracks."

"I'm with you," Lonegan said. He and Bridge and Pee Wee bolted for the door. Bridge kicked it open and disappeared outside, followed by Pee Wee. Lonegan hesitated on his way out, and leered at Fargo.

"Still say you look like Skye Fargo," he said.

"Name's Parsons," Fargo said, and suddenly he remembered why Deke Lonegan knew him.

He aimed his pistol at Fargo's head and cocked the trigger. This was too much for Corny, who'd had enough killing to last several lifetimes. He crumpled to the floor in a dead faint.

"Ought to kill you here and now anyway," Lonegan said. "My gut tells me you're a-gonna be a thorn in my side someday soon."

"Guts can be wrong," Fargo responded.

"Let's get movin'," Al Bridge called from outside. Pee Wee and Flat-Eye had already mounted up and were chomping at the bit to kick the dust of San Angelo off their heels.

Deke Lonegan knew there were only a few precious seconds remaining before the law would descend on them like locusts in a cornfield. Killing this tall man would have to wait. Lonegan turned and made for his horse and was about to mount up when a skinny mongrel trotted up, bearing its teeth and growling. He sank his choppers into Lonegan's foot, but before they could penetrate leather, Lonegan shot the dog in the head, the cur's body flipping into the air and landing in a dead heap.

Lonegan and his men put spurs to flanks and galloped off down Main Street, firing at anything that dared to move.

As he rode off, Flat-Eye looked down at the dead dog and sadly remarked, "There go good breakfast."

Fargo leapt to his feet, his heart pounding in his chest. Deke Lonegan. Fargo cursed himself for not remembering right away.

"Get your friend on his feet," he said to Ferdie. "I may be wrong, but I think we're gonna get blamed for this."

Ferdie stared dumbly at Fargo, who was checking the fat banker for signs of life.

"We . . . us . . . I . . ." Ferdie looked at the dead bodies of the banker and his wife, shock setting in and with a powerful vengeance. His legs felt as though they were heavier than lead and glued to the floor. His friend was much better off; he was out like a cold mackerel on the floor. Neither of them had ever seen dead people before, much less dead people who were killed before their very eyes.

Fargo quickly examined the banker's wife, knowing she was well beyond help. He looked up at Ferdie, whose eyes were glazed over and heavy-lidded.

"You ain't going to faint, are you boy?" Ferdie dimly heard Fargo say, then the tall man was up and screaming straight into his face. Ferdie heard only every third or fourth word through the shocked haze in his head, unaware that he was weaving unsteadily until Fargo grabbed him by the shoulders.

". . . blamed . . . killin's . . . catch us . . . hanging party . . . can't explain . . . get going . . ."

Ferdie blinked rapidly. Fargo could see that he wasn't quite getting through to the youth. He slapped Ferdie back and forth three times until the kid came back to the same world as everyone else.

"Can you understand what I'm saying to you, boy?" Fargo said to Ferdie as calmly as was possible under the circumstances.

Ferdie nodded, swallowing hard and dry.

"Two, maybe three people are dead," Fargo said to him. "And we just happened to be in the same bank where it happened. Maybe they'll believe we had no hand in it, but maybe they won't."

"But . . . we didn't." Ferdie stammered. "Who were those men?"

"Deke Lonegan and his gang," Fargo said, and went to Corny, kneeling beside him. He slapped him gently on the face until the skinny kid started to stir. "Ain't seen that murdering little devil since Dodge. Thought he'd be long dead by now. Who could've figured?"

Fargo brought Corny around. The boy was moaning softly now, but still a fair piece from being fully awake.

"Are those people dead?" Ferdie asked.

"If they ain't, they're doing a damn fine imitation," Fargo said, dragging Corny to his feet. "Snap out of it, goddamn it!"

"We didn't kill them," Ferdie said.

Fargo pushed Corny into a chair, then gave Ferdie another hard slap, mostly because he felt like it. "You dumb little shit," Fargo snapped at him. "We came in here to rob a bank because you wanted to. I set it up with him—" he pointed to the dead man, "to let you boys have your stupid fun."

"You mean," Ferdie stammered, "we weren't really robbing this bank?"

"Why the hell do you think it was so goddamn easy!" Fargo barked angrily. "Trouble is, I don't think the good folks of San Angelo got much hankering to believe it, especially since the only ones who knew are laying here dead."

"But surely everyone will understand," Ferdie said weakly.

"Only thing they'll understand," Fargo said, loading bullets into the chamber of his Colt, "is the hangman's rope around our gullets."

"Won't running away make it worse?" Ferdie asked.

"Most likely," Fargo said. "But I don't think we'll get the chance to explain our side of it. Hell, I wouldn't believe it myself."

Fargo lifted Corny by the collar and pushed him toward the door.

10

Fargo flew out the back door and saw a dozen or so very big men, the biggest San Angelo had to offer from the looks of it, running toward the bank sporting all kinds of guns, big and small. Fargo reached inside and grabbed Ferdie by the collar, who in turn grabbed Corny by his sleeve. Fargo pulled them both out the door and shouted, "Move like your asses are on fire."

Fargo started unhitching the Ovaro just as the first round of gunshots pierced the morning, kicking up dust inches from where he stood. He mounted and spurred his horse, then saw his new friends standing frozen in fear like two wooden Indians.

"Mount up, boys!" Fargo yelled, as more gunshots peppered around him. The dozen men had turned into two dozen. Fargo was glad for the moment that he'd chosen a couple of sturdy horses for this particular job. "We got company."

They looked at Fargo stupidly; the gravity of the situation still wasn't registering in their addled brains. Fargo fired a shot over their heads. They snapped out of it instantly.

"You boys wanted to be desperadoes," Fargo shouted. "You got it in spades."

Ferdie and Corny got the message. They dashed to their horses. Ferdie started unhitching his mount when the sound of a bullet roared inches above his ears and blew the hat from his head. Half a second later he was fully mounted like he'd been shot out of a cannon. Corny mounted at the same time, though he forgot to unhitch his horse. He spurred the animal, who was unaware he was still tethered to the hitching post. The horse reared up two feet, just enough for Corny to roll over backwards, heels over head, and crash to the street.

Fargo cursed and galloped back amidst the increasing gunshots toward Corny, who was getting unsteadily to his feet. The gods were, for the moment, on their side, as none of the arriving gunfire was finding its target.

"Your hand!" Fargo bellowed, and swooped down on the boy. Corny stuck his hand out—this was what they did in *Great Western Tales*—and just like in all the stories, Fargo grabbed it. Corny felt himself lifted off his feet and deposited squarely behind the big man, coming down hard on the saddle. Fargo spurred the Ovaro and rode like hellfire toward the edge of town. The angry sound of gunfire was nothing new to him. Fargo was relieved to see that Ferdie was right behind him.

Corny grabbed the back of Fargo's belt and held on for dear life, screaming, "How much trouble are we in, Mr. Fargo?"

"Those rifles you hear ain't exactly blowin' kisses," Fargo yelled back.

For reasons he couldn't quite figure, Corny felt like he wanted to cry. Above the noise of galloping hooves and gunfire, he shouted at Fargo, "Ferdie talked me into this. I really wanted to go to Paris this summer."

"If it makes you feel any better, I wish you'd gone to Paris too," Fargo responded.

Fargo estimated that they had a good ten-minute lead before a posse could be formed. Bank robberies weren't as common as they'd once been in this part of the state, and the townies were off their guard. Fargo knew he had to be careful not to catch up with Deke Lonegan and his boys, who were only minutes ahead of them. Best to head east once out of town, and hope the posse picked up Deke Lonegan's trail instead of their own. Lonegan would head south, to Mexico. Any other direction held too many problems for that bunch.

Fargo allowed himself a quick look back. Ferdie was keeping apace with them, but barely managed to stay on the saddle. What he lacked in horsemanship he made up for in determination to stay alive. Fargo was almost impressed.

"Your friend could almost pass for a Westerner," Fargo said to Corny.

"The way this day is going," Corny replied, "I think he'll settle for being alive."

They were walking their horses through the patches of mesquite and rocky West Texas soil, the early afternoon sun beating down on them. The posse had split in two a mile out of town, where Deke Lonegan and Fargo's trails had parted. The trail dust of six to nine riders on the horizon behind them kept Fargo pushing harder and harder, until their horses were foaming at the mouth with exhaustion—along with the two boys. Fargo only rode them hard for another two miles, when their pursuers faded from sight.

Only now would Fargo let them walk the horses long enough to cool them off, then they'd mount up and ride hard again. The next water was at least six mils due east.

"Why are we walking when we could be riding?" Ferdie wanted to know. "How can we stay ahead of them if we walk?"

"The horses need to cool down for a spell," Fargo said. "I told you already, they'll die on us if we don't. Our friends from town are doing the same thing if they're smart, and they are. Don't forget—my mount is carrying two, because your friend was stupid enough to lose his own horse."

For his part, Corny was content to walk instead of ride. His insides felt like jelly. Riding horses at breakneck speed wasn't much fun. "I heard that, Fargo," Corny piped up. "I don't take any cotton to that kind of talk."

"The only cotton is the big wad between your ears," Fargo said testily. "Both of you. You couldn't be happy with just getting drunk and laid, no, not you two beanheads. You wanted to rob a bank, and I was dumb enough to help you. Sweet Jesus, what the hell was I thinking?"

"You were thinking about the money we paid you," Ferdie said.

Fargo cast an angry glance at Ferdie but found himself at a loss for words. Instead, he wanted to kick this little twerp's ass from Texas to China. Fargo hated when other people were right.

"Maybe I was," Fargo said. "And I've earned every penny. I didn't guarantee another band of prairie rats could come in and spoil your fun."

Ferdie chewed nervously on a weed he'd plucked a ways back. It tasted terrible, but chewing weeds was what folks did in the West. He was scared, right down to his socks. Fargo had to told him that there were men not far behind them who wanted to stretch his neck like warm taffy, and Ferdie believed it. Three people were dead, partly because he and Corny wanted to play cowboy, and now there was hell to pay. He and Corny needed Fargo more than he needed them, of that there was no argument. This was the tall man's domain, and he impressed Ferdie as a man who knew how to stay alive and healthy.

"What do we do now?" Corny asked. It seemed a fair question.

"Been studying on that," Fargo said. "I reckon our best bet is to turn south and track Deke Lonegan and his boys, get the money back, and bring the guilty parties to justice, so's to clear our names."

"You mean you actually know the man who robbed the bank?" Ferdie asked, impressed.

"Yes."

"He did seem to know you, now that I think about it," Corny said.

"Tried to cheat me in a card game in Shreveport some years back," Fargo said. "Hard to forget a man when he lays down four aces and you're holdin' two of your own. Took off a piece of his ear with a slug from a forty-five. Been seein' his ugly face plastered on wanted posters as far west as Tucson ever since."

"Seeing how they went in one direction and we in another," Ferdie said dryly, "how do you propose we catch them?"

"I just said that's what we needed to do," Fargo said. "Didn't say anything about having a plan."

"Wouldn't it be better if Ferdie and I just went home to New York?" Corny asked.

"Yes," Ferdie said. "An excellent suggestion."

"Three people are dead back there," Fargo said. "Or ain't that important to you city folk?"

"It wasn't our fault those people are dead," Ferdie said.

"It is in the eyes of the law," Fargo said. "If it was just the money we were discussing here, that'd be one thing. I'd say so long, boys, and send you home with a clear conscience. But some good folks are dead, and we played a part in it by just being there. Until we can bring in Deke Lonegan and his boys or die trying, we'll have blood on our hands, and that ain't something I'm quite prepared to live with. Yeah, I've killed, but it was always folks that were in dire need of a good killing. No," he went on, "Deke Lonegan tarnished my good name, and I got to polish it back up. And you two greenhorn city-shit peckerheads are gonna help me. You came to Texas to be real desperadoes, and now you're getting your money's worth."

"Get us to the nearest train station," Ferdie said, "and you'll be handsomely rewarded. Our daddies—"

Fargo shook his head. "My innards tell me I can't," he said. "Besides, the law will nail you both faster than a fart in a tailwind the second you board a train. Way I see it, you got no options but sticking close. Without me, you'll die like gophers in a rattlesnake pit, and your rich daddies can't buy you out of that."

"If we could at least send them a telegram, then maybe—" Ferdie began.

"We ain't got time for maybes," Fargo said. "Not judging by that dust getting closer by the minute." He pointed to the south where the posse was kicking up a huge brown cloud of the Texas prairie. "Let's ride," he said.

Ferdie needed no prodding, climbing onto his bay and putting spurts to flanks. He was learning. Fargo saddled up and pulled Corny onto the saddle behind him. They tore off hell bent for leather. Ferdie bounced in the saddle, gripping the reins and trying hard, as before, not to tumble off the horse.

"Where exactly are we headed?" Corny yelled above the pounding of the horses' hooves. He held onto Fargo's belt for dear life with one hand, holding his hat on his head with the other.

Fargo yelled back, "Got to get us some provisions. I know a little trading post not far from here. Owner don't ask no questions. These horses need grain and rest."

"But the posse—" Corny started.

"They won't follow us for long, not where we're headed," Fargo shouted.

"And where would that be Mr. Fargo?" Corny wanted to know.

"Indian Territory," Fargo responded.

"Indians?" Corny cried. "I thought they were all on reservations in Oklahoma Territory. That's what it said in the newspapers."

"Some of 'em didn't take kindly to the government's generous offer," Fargo yelled back.

"But what about Deke Lonegan and his gang?" Corny asked.

Fargo spurred his horse even harder, almost losing Corny in the process. The posse wasn't about to give up anytime soon, not that Fargo could blame them. They wouldn't waste time on a hanging, either—they'd blow Fargo and his pals right out of their saddles given the chance.

"Deke'll head for Mexico if he's got half an ounce of brains," Fargo bellowed. "He'll have to go through Comanche country to get there. We'll cross paths with the sumbitch if we beat this posse and our luck holds out."

"I hope my ass holds out," Corny commented.

Ferdie was lagging behind them; the kid was just too green for this type of pursuit. He was barely managing the horse. He was slowing them down. Fargo pulled his pistol and fired off two shots. Ferdie's bay reared up in fear while the boy grabbed the saddlehorn and bucked up half a foot off the leather. His eyes bulged hideously in stark terror as he bounced around, but he managed to stay on horseback.

"Just hold on tight and pray for your heathen soul, boy!" Fargo shouted back at Ferdie.

11

Cockeye Jackson had a fat Indian wife and six half-breed children ranging in age from three to sixteen. Cockeye had been a South Texas fixture for as long as anyone could remember. He was a tall, big-bellied man with a white beard and eyeballs that went in opposite directions, hence his nickname. Nobody seemed to know his real first name; he'd been Cockeye forever.

Mesquite and chinaberries surrounded the desolate mud and stick structure, an oasis in the flat South Texas country. Cockeye's was the only place to get a bottle of whiskey or a slab of bacon for sixty square miles, and he didn't much care who his customers were, outlaw or otherwise, as long as they paid cash. Nobody gave Cockeye any trouble. His two oldest sons, despite their youth, were crack shots with both rifle and pistol. Few tried to rob Cockeye Jackson and lived to tell about it. The hill behind the trading post, with a dozen crudely made crosses tramped into the soil, was testament to this fact.

Fargo and his companions walked up to the bar, such as it was, a plank of wood resting on two barrels. They were caked with dust and dog tired. Fargo wanted nothing more than some whiskey to wash down the clogged dirt in the back of his throat. Ferdie and Corny wanted three weeks of uninterrupted slumber. They'd ridden for over a day, eating little and resting even less.

Mrs. Jackson rose from a rocking chair to greet them. She was a stout, rawboned Comanche woman with a hard-chiseled, expressionless face and black hair worn in tight braids. Her two oldest, bad hombres to be sure, sat in chairs near the fire.

"Hello, Skye Fargo," she said.

"Hello, Liddiflower."

The stout Indian woman went to Fargo and affectionately patted his cheek.

"Been too long, Fargo," she said. "Cockeye, me, we miss you."

"You look as beautiful as ever, Liddiflower," Fargo smiled. "Seeing you, my heart flaps its wings like the hawk."

"Cut some crap, Fargo," Liddiflower said. "Are you in trouble again?"

"I suspect I am," Fargo said, looking toward his dirty traveling companions. "These are my friends, Liddiflower." He pointed to Corny. "This one I call He Who Dry-Heaves."

Corny blanched as Liddiflower turned her cold-iron gaze on him. He tipped his hat and said, "Ma'am."

Fargo motioned to Ferdie. He said to Liddiflower, "This is Young Man Who Wets His Pants."

Ferdie tried to grin and managed only to look sick. This Indian woman could have doubled for the wooden one who stood proudly outside of Kaminsky's Cigar Store on Second Avenue. He said, "How. I mean, hi."

Liddiflower checked them over. She didn't seem too impressed. She said, "Snot noses."

"I think you've got the situation pegged," Fargo agreed.

Liddiflower went behind the bar. She pulled out a bottle that held some rich brown liquid. "Whiskey?" she asked Fargo?

"Whiskey," Fargo said to her. She hesitated until Fargo slapped a silver dollar onto the bar, then she put three dirty shot glasses down in front of them.

"Got any ginger beer?" Corny asked.

The fat Indian lady shook her head, scooping up the silver dollar. She poured each of them a shot, then corked the bottle. Fargo downed his and signaled for another. Ferdie and his friend sniffed theirs, took a few tentative sips, and grimaced in distaste.

"How's Cockeye?" Fargo asked her, and downed his second drink.

"He live still," Liddiflower said.

"I need to see him," Fargo said.

Liddiflower disappeared into the back room. A minute

or two later, the tall, barrel-chested man came out yawning, pulling up his suspenders. Cockeye's huge gut jutted out, covered by a filthy undershirt.

Cockeye rubbed his sleepy eyes and focused on a very dusty Skye Fargo. His grumpy frown turned into an ear-to-ear grin.

"Skye Fargo, as I live and breathe," Cockeye Jackson said, "Ain't seen your miserable butt in a coon's age."

"It's been awhile, Cockeye," Fargo said. Ferdie and Corny had no part in this reunion of two old friends, and respectfully kept their mouths shut.

Cockeye went behind the bar and pulled out a second bottle. He grabbed a glass for himself and poured two shots, one into his glass and one into Fargo's, ignoring the two whippersnappers with him.

Fargo and Cockeye clinked glasses.

"To luck," Fargo said.

"Luck," Cockeye responded.

They downed their drinks, as befitted the toast.

Cockeye poured them each another. "Where you been keepin' yourself, Fargo?"

"Here and there," Fargo said. He sipped his whiskey. This stuff was a vast improvement on the cheap hooch Cockeye's Indian wife had served them.

"Prob'ly don't remember my family," Cockeye said, motioning to the two beefy half-breed boys sitting near the fire. "Them's my sons, Hiram and Walker."

"Named your boys for a bottle of whiskey, did you?" Fargo asked.

"Would've named 'em for my old daddy," Cockeye said, "but I never made his acquaintance."

"Stands to reason," Fargo said.

Cockeye examined Fargo a little more closely. He said, "You look like a man what's got hisself some trouble, Skye."

Fargo nodded warily. "I could say I didn't," he said, "but who'd believe me?"

"I might," Cockeye said. "We go back some years, Skye. Still remember the day we took turns poppin' off Mexicans like wild turkeys in a meadow."

"We just forgot which side we were on, Cockeye," Fargo said.

"Forgot my ass," Cockeye said. "You always had a talent for pickin' the right side, Fargo."

"Used to," Fargo said.

"We rode with some mean sidewinders, old son, but you were never one of their kind," Cockeye said. "You been walkin' the straight and narrow forever, friend. You're in trouble now, it's for a good reason."

"Nothing but the best for me, Cockeye," Fargo said, and took a drink. "Deke Lonegan killed some folks back in San Angelo, and it's our asses gettin' the heat."

"Deke Lonegan?" Cockeye asked. "You sure?"

"Sure as I'm sippin' your best hooch, Cockeye," Fargo said. "How's things around here?"

Liddiflower came out and started babbling in a language that was half-Indian and half-Mex. Cockeye listened attentively to her for a minute. He turned to Fargo and said, "The missus knows the way of the Comanche. She says Circlin' Hawk is off the reservation and just itchin' for trouble."

The Indian woman let loose with another two minutes of chatter, looking over at Fargo now and then accusingly. Cockeye nodded, saying nothing. His wife finished speaking, then went and sat down in a rocking chair near the fire.

Cockeye said, "Don't mind the missus. She don't mean to be cross. Just in her nature."

"No offense taken," Fargo said. "Circlin' Hawk, you say?"

Cockeye nodded. "Him and forty of his braves came through here a week ago Tuesday and took dam near ever' last ounce of whiskey I had. Wasn't about to refuse 'em."

"Did he ask about me?" Fargo wanted to know.

"As a matter of fact, your name did come up," Cockeye said. "You two got some serious bad blood twixt y'all."

"Excuse me," Corny piped up, "but who is this Circlin' Hawk?"

It was the first time either of Fargo's new friends had spoken. Fargo turned to Cockeye. "Meet my new partners, Ferdinand and Cornelius, two of the most feared outlaws east of nowhere."

"Pleased to meet any friends of Skye Fargo's," Cockeye said. "You boys want a drink?"

"Yes," Corny said.

"Sure," answered Ferdie.

"No," Fargo said. "We still got some ridin' to do today, and I don't want nothing that'll slow us up. Hell, cold sober you can barely stick to your saddles."

"*You're* drinking," Ferdie said pointedly.

"Yeah, and I'm gonna keep drinkin' till I don't feel like it anymore," he said, reaching for the bottle. He poured himself and Cockeye another.

"Gonna be a posse swinging down through here shortly," Fargo said to Cockeye. "Where's Circlin' Hawk keeping himself?"

"Word is he and his braves are holed up around Three Fingers," Cockeye said. "You thinkin' about payin' him a visit?"

"Gonna try not to," Fargo said. "But I figure the posse won't follow us down into Indian Territory."

"If Circlin' Hawk catches y'all, you won't have to worry about no posse," Cockeye said. "His pecker is up. And you're about the last person he wants to see, Fargo."

"I'll have to risk it," Fargo said. "We got to get that money back from Deke Lonegan if we're to clear our names. I'm too old for any owlhoot trail."

"Just who exactly is this Circlin' Hawk?" Ferdie asked.

"As mean an Indian what ever lived," Cockeye said. "Meaner still when he's got hisself a snootful of firewater. You boys just hope you never make the pleasure of his acquaintance, less you want to be usin' your eyeballs as earrings."

"And we're going . . . where he is?" Corny asked.

"I think so," Fargo said.

"Why is this Circlin' Hawk mad at you, Mr. Fargo?" Ferdie asked.

"It's a long story," Fargo replied.

Fargo finished his drink and hitched up his britches. He said to Cockeye, "We'll be needin' some supplies, bacon and coffee and bullets and such. A bottle, too, if Circlin' Hawk didn't take it all."

"I keep a few stashed away," Cockeye said. "Guess I can spare one.'

"Gonna need a mount for him," Fargo said, pointing to Corny. Corny pulled a wad of bills from his pocket and started counting some off onto the bar.

Ten minutes later, they were loading the horses up with supplies. For fifty dollars, Cockeye furnished Corny with an old, but sturdy chestnut and an ancient saddle. "She ain't much to look at," Cockeye said, "but she'll get y'all to where you're goin'."

Corny said to Ferdie, "He's taking us where Indians live. I don't like this, partner. Remember what happened to Big Jim Kane in that book *Six-Gun Justice,* when the redskins captured him?"

Ferdie looked a little green around the gills. "They cut off his eyelids and buried him in the sand. And then the buzzards swooped down and—" His voice trailed off. Fear lodged in his belly like a lump of coal. "I don't like it either, but, we're in big trouble, Corny, more than we ever could have hoped to find. We got to see this one through, whatever the outcome."

"We might get ourselves killed, Ferdie," Corny said.

Ferdie nodded. "We might."

Corny looked down at the ground and kicked some dirt. "If we do," he said, "and I hope we don't—but if we do, I just want to say, Ferdie . . . I liked being your friend. It was fun."

Ferdie flushed. "It's been a real kick in the ass, partner."

"Maybe I'll see you when we get to heaven," Corny said.

"I think there's a rule against raisin' hell in heaven," Ferdie grinned. "Besides, how will I know you?"

"I'll be the one wearin' the oversized hat." A tear leaked from his eye. He never knew what true, shit-eating fear was until this very moment. Life and death situations were something entirely new to him.

"Relax, partner," Ferdie said, hating to see his friend fighting tears. "I'm sure Fargo will save our ham."

Corny blew his nose on his sleeve and said, "Bacon. Save our bacon."

Fargo mounted up. "Let's make tracks, ladies. Time's a wastin'."

"I hate that expression," Ferdie grumbled, climbing onto his horse.

Fargo reined in his horse. "Thanks for everything, Cockeye," Fargo called to his old friend. "I'll be seein' you."

Fargo, Corny, and Ferdie galloped off. A dark band of thunderheads were rolling in from the east. Cockeye called back, "I do hope so, Skye Fargo. May the Good Lord stop whatever he's doin' and look after y'all."

Cockeye watched them melt into the horizon, and wondered if he'd ever see Fargo again. He wouldn't bet good money on it.

12

"This isn't good," Corny said.

Indeed it wasn't. No less than thirty braves, on horseback, were lined up on the ridge parallel to where Fargo and his friends now rode. The Indians sat patiently, as if they had all the time in the world to ambush the three of them. Fargo tightened his grip on the reins but didn't spur his horse into a gallop, not yet. If these were Circling Hawk's braves, they'd soon swoop down on the three of them when they were good and ready. Comanche liked to play their victims like a tomcat tormenting a cornered mouse.

"If those injuns attack," Fargo told his companions, "you boys are on your own. I'll ride off to divert them. You boys head in another direction, and I'll circle back for you."

"Do you think they will?" Ferdie asked, already dreading the answer.

"Yes," Fargo said. "When I holler, you boys haul ass and haul it as fast as you can."

They trotted on for a bit, then Fargo cried, "Yee-haw!" and spurred his horse into a hard gallop. Ferdie and Corny followed suit. Behind them, they could hear the defiant war cries of the Comanche, who were kicking up huge brown clouds of dust as they up and gave pursuit. The fact that the Comanche were sporting some very fine rifles was not lost on Fargo.

He'd hoped to make it across this territory unmolested by the Comanche and had journeyed several miles north in the hopes of avoiding them. The odds of them actually encountering the braves were slightly better than winning a Juarez faro game, but worth risking nonetheless. Fargo cursed silently—he hated to gamble and lose. But lose he had, and he was determined to survive his folly.

Corny, in an attempt to keep up with his friends, gripped the reins and spurred the chestnut trying not to bounce out of the saddle. The war cries of the Comanche seemed to grow louder and louder behind him. Moments later, gunshots echoed out. Both Ferdie and Corny realized with new horror that the Indians were shooting at them.

"Oh God-oh-God-oh-God," Corny sobbed as bullets kicked up dust eddies only inches ahead of him. He crouched down lower, his butt bouncing up and down off the saddle painfully. He spurred the horse harder, and for a brief time he felt a tinge of hope that he'd actually outrun the savages. Then his stomach lurched upwards as the chestnut took some lead in his left flank and went down, flopping over sideways. Corny went flying through the morning like a cannnonball, then careened off a particularly large rock, and rolled into a heap.

Ferdie was vaguely aware that he'd lost his friend and ventured a look back. Corny was lying flat on his back, motionless, his horse dying. The Comanche would be upon him in seconds.

Ferdie could not leave his friend to die at the hands of these merciless red savages. Fargo was, Ferdie saw, oblivious to Corny's plight, galloping into the horizon like a madman. Ferdie jerked the horse's reins and went to save his friend.

Twenty or so yards before he could get to Corny, Ferdie felt something rip through his arm, which then exploded with pain. He tumbled off his horse and crashed to the ground grunting. Corny sat up, shook his head, and saw Ferdie lying flat on his back, his arm spurting blood. He scrambled on his hands and knees over to Ferdie, bullets tearing chunks off the rocks on either side of him. He reached Ferdie and scooped him up in his arms, cradling him.

"You're hit," Corny said.

"I know," Ferdie said breathlessly, his face the color of new cheese. "It sure doesn't tickle."

"Here," Corny said, grabbing a dirty handkerchief out of his pocket and putting it on the wound in Ferdie's shoulder. "They just grazed you."

"Truth be told, I've felt better," Ferdie said, growing paler and paler, trying to suck some air into his tortured lungs.

"I think we're in deep, dark trouble," Corny said as the hard-riding wave of Comanche descended on them.

Ferdie, lying in his friend's arms, looked up at the angry Indians. They were more frightening than any he'd seen in some picture book—naked to the waist, baked golden brown from the sun, their features more than visible through the half-inch of dirt on their faces, soulless black eyes peering down at the two *wihios*.

The Comanche dismounted and surrounded their white captives, fifteen Winchesters aimed at their heads. Ferdie and Corny lay motionless as the Indians suddenly parted like the Red Sea and another Indian strode confidently through the crowd and stood over them.

This Indian had a wide, fleshy face painted with red and yellow stripes on his cheeks. He was short and squat and more bald than an onion. At first glance he looked no more a threat than a mosquito, but there was something akin to anger and hatred in his ink-black eyes that put fear into the hearts of most men. He was the leader make no mistake.

The leader handed his rifle to one of his braves and peered down at his new captives. His stony face remained impassive as he sized them up. Neither was the white man he wanted, but he was certain that the man he sought had been among them.

"Think they're going to kill us?" Corny asked.

"I don't know. Maybe they're friendly Indians," Ferdie said hopefully.

"They don't look very friendly," Corny said. "I really wish we'd gone to Paris."

"I'd settle for the Bowery right now," Ferdie said.

The bald Indian said something to the other braves in a language neither Ferdie nor Corny could understand. The other braves made a circle around them. Ferdie noticed now that these redskins were oddly dressed, much different from the ones in the picture books. Some wore white men's hats; one wore a dapper black derby atop greasy black hair tied into matching braids. Others were wearing blue jeans tucked into moccasins, some sported leather vests, and almost all were carrying guns that were definitely made in the United States.

The Indians were laughing and pointing at their two captives. One Indian, taller than a redwood tree with no teeth, rotting gums, and a long, jagged scar from his left eye down to the corner of his mouth, suddenly loomed up over Ferdie. The scar gave his face a droopy, sinister look. Ferdie, despite the heat, shivered. The ugly redskin was smiling at him, but there was little mirth in it. Then the giant produced a knife that looked to be roughly the size of Rhode Island. Sun glinted off the blade as the Indian snapped his wrist and a second later the blade was embedded in the soil half an inch from Ferdie's crotch.

The Indian reached into his pants and pulled out an impossibly huge penis, waving it in his hand for one and all to see. The other Indians laughed as though this was the funniest spectacle they'd ever witnessed.

"I think this means trouble," Ferdie heard Corny mutter.

The leader was deep in serious conference with several of his friends, and didn't seem to care that his braves were tormenting the *wihios*.

"Why is he doing that?" Corny asked his friend. He hadn't been this scared in at least two hours. A hanging party was one thing—a person could at least speak English to them—but Indians were different. The tall Indian continued shaking his manhood at them.

"I don't know," Ferdie commented, "but somehow I don't think this is the Indian version of Punch and Judy."

The Indian took two steps forward, straddling Ferdie. The leader turned and snapped angrily at the tall Indian, who put his manhood back into its appropriate spot, then slunk away to rejoin the other braves.

Cornie and Ferdie breathed a collective sigh of relief, until the bald Indian walked over and stood over Ferdie himself. He was wearing filthy blue jeans, but was naked otherwise. His chest was brown from the sun and hard enough to be chiseled from stone. He started to unbutton his blue jeans.

Ferdie said, "I feel like a bride on the maid's day off."

The leader kicked Ferdie in the side, then just as quickly connected the toe of his moccasin with Ferdie's jaw. Ferdie saw stars explode in his head as it snapped back into the South Texas dirt.

The leader let loose with a stream of yellow piss that sailed over Ferdie's inert form and splattered into the ground inches from the top of his head. Ferdie watched the piss sail over his head and thought *he's trying to humiliate me.* What better way to degrade a man than to urinate in his general direction?

After the leader finished his business he flicked the last few drops onto Ferdie's face. He buttoned up and turned to his braves, yelling something at them. Half a dozen of them descended on Ferdie and Corny, dragging them to their feet and off to parts unknown.

"Oh-God-oh-God," Corny kept yelping. "This isn't fair . . . we're on vacation!"

"It's out of his hands now, partner," Ferdie said, sounding almost resigned to his fate. "Whatever happens, happens."

"What if I don't like it?" Corny asked, while a dozen grimy Indian hands forced him towards a bonfire being built by the redskins, who were tossing whatever they could find in the way of twigs and dried leaves into the flames.

"I don't know," Ferdie said, and got six solid kicks in the legs from his captors. His knees buckled, but he was propelled forward by the force of six Indians to the bonfire. Corny was similarly dragged closer to the hot flames.

"Is this fire for us?" Corny asked.

"I hope not," Ferdie said.

The Indians tossed them to the ground like handfuls of pebbles, then yanked off the *wihios'* boots, a bunch of the Indians competing for the expensive, hand-crafted goodies. Knives were brought out and the fights began in earnest, the young braves slashing each other over the booty.

Their leader could have cared less. He barked orders at his men. The redskins divided up their captives' belongings kicking the *wihios* in every part of their bodies.

Ferdie's and Corny's hands were tied behind their backs. Two braves attended to the task, getting no resistance from the prisoners.

The Comanche already had two wooden poles pounded into the ground behind what looked to be a large mound of dirt. Ferdie and Corny were then tied to the posts, their hands behind their backs.

Ferdie whispered to Corny, "Remember that part in *Six Guns to Apache Pass*? What did Rip Washburn do when the Indians captured him?"

"He chopped his arm off and hit himself over the head with it," Corny said. "So they would think he was crazy."

"No, that was in *Shadow Riders of the Brazos*," Ferdie said. "When the Banning brothers ride into the Comanche ambush and—"

Corny interrupted him, "Why does that big pile of dirt look like it's moving?" He nodded his head toward the mound of dirt a few feet in front of where they were now securely staked to the wooden poles.

Ferdie looked. Indeed, the mound appeared to writhe in a sea of red. An Indian appeared before them, clutching a can of some kind. He started pouring thick black gunk—Ferdie dimly realized it was molasses—over their heads and bodies. The Indian disappeared. The others were hunkering around the fire and cooking up some rabbit meat, chattering and laughing in anticipation of the afternoon's entertainment.

"Ants!" Ferdie gasped, the horror of their situation blossoming in his brain. "It's an anthill. They splashed molasses on our pants so the ants will eat us alive."

"Just like in *Blazing Guns on the Chisholm Trail*," Corny said.

"You wrong," said a voice behind them. The bald Indian—the one in charge, appeared before them. He waved a dog-eared, yellowing dime novel at them. "It was *Showdown at Rattlesnake Gulch*. Where you think I get the idea?"

Ferdie and Corny exchanged puzzled glances.

"The white man's words portray us as little more than mad dogs," the bald Indian said, tapping his finger on the book. "And his prose stink."

"You speak very good English," Ferdie said.

"To deal with the white man, one must lie as well as the white man," the chief said. "I learn to read on the reservation. Your Eastern writers know nothing of the Comanche and their ways. Their stories have no souls. Take much literary license with truth."

"Guess I never thought about it," Ferdie said.

The chief tossed the dime novel into the fire. "I am Circling Hawk," he said to the boys.

"He's the one they were talking about in that trading post," Ferdie whispered to his friend.

Circling Hawk said to his captives, "Your faces free of wrinkles from sun and your hands are smoother than a piglet's flesh." He leaned in closer. "You boys not from around here, are you?"

"We're from New York City," Ferdie explained.

"We came out here to have some Western adventure and excitement," Corny added.

"You get plenty here," Circling Hawk said. "It is Skye Fargo you ride with?"

They both nodded. "We paid him money to help us be real cowboys," Ferdie said.

"And now he ran off and left us at your mercy," Corny said.

Circling Hawk almost smiled. He said, "No. Fargo is very near. I can feel his bad medicine in my bones."

Ferdie glanced nevously at the anthill. The big red insects were making their way closer to him and Corny. The molasses was a pungent, effective lure.

"Are you going to kill us, Mr. Hawk?" Corny said, also noting that the bugs were creeping in formation toward him and Ferdie and their syrup-splattered britches.

"Fire ants, many, many of them in mound," Circling Hawk said. "They will pick your bones clean before the sun sets. Skye Fargo hear your screams, curse himself for the coward that he is."

"It sounds like you're mad at him," Ferdie said.

"He owe me money," Circling Hawk said, and barked an Indian command at his braves. Two of them rushed over to the huge anthill and began poking it with big sticks. Thousands of angry red ants streamed out and swarmed their way toward Ferdie and Corny.

"They prefer to work at night," Circling Hawk said, backing cautiously away from the red onslaught. "Hot sun makes them very mad. You suffer very long time, I think."

"I'm sure we can work this out," Ferdie said, panic seeping into his voice as the first few critters scurried over his feet and headed straight up his leg. "Whatever Mr. Fargo owes you, we can wire our fathers and—"

"Wihio miss point," Pissing Hawk said. "Skye Fargo dishonor Circling Hawk. You, his friends, must pay the price."

"Mr. Hawk—" Ferdie began, but was cut off by an ear-splitting scream from his friend. The red ants were cascading up Corny's legs under his pants. Corny was kicking his legs futility to shake them off. A moment later, Ferdie felt the first painful stings of the marauding ants as they sank their stingers into his calves.

Ferdie let out a fine scream of his own, and the Indians laughed louder as they munched on their rabbit meat. Hundreds of tiny knives stung Ferdie and Corny's legs; huge clumps of red ants pooled on the molasses puddles at their feet.

Corny screamed, and wailed.

The ants continued their upward march, spreading out under the boys' shirts and across their chests. The ants' stings covered every last inch of their bodies. Corny whimpered in pain, while Ferdie tried to swallow his screams so as not to give this Indian chief the satisfaction of hearing him cry out. For some crazy reason, this seemed important.

The ants stung their way up to the boys' faces, systematically ripping and stinging their flesh. Corny continued screaming, oblivious now to the legions of red ants that tried to crawl into his open mouth. Ferdie could feel the little red devils nipping at his neck and scalp, the bites and stings on his chest and legs already a foregone conclusion.

The late afternoon wind whipped through their hair but could not stop the hungry horde. Ferdie and Corny squirmed in agony against the ropes that bound their wrists to the wooden posts. Corny was hysterical, the fire ants attacking every last inch of his skin. Ferdie surrendered to the pain and let loose with a pitiful howl as the red devils tried to devour him from toe to head. He remembered the legions of termites that invaded the family home in Gramercy Park, swarming all out from behind the kitchen walls. Elsie, the fat Negro cook, was helpless to stop them. Ferdie remembered the little flying bastards descending on his breakfast, in his hair, up his nose. He remembered running out of the big kitchen, screaming, trying to brush the termites away.

That was bad, but this was much worse. These ants meant business. And at the moment, business was very good. Had his hands not been tied so tightly to the wooden post, Ferdie would have sank to his knees and let the ants have their way with him.

"Eaten by ants," Ferdie said. "What a stupid way to die."

"Don't take this personally," Corny said, "but I hate your guts."

Despite his pain, Ferdie said, "What did I do?"

"This is all your fault," Corny said. "Almost getting me thrown out of school, making my father hate me, coming here to live out some stupid dream we had no right dreaming in the first place."

"I admit I made some mistakes," Ferdie said to his friend, ants nipping at every part of him. "And yes, we're being eaten alive by ants, but that's no reason to hate me."

The ants were nipping at Corny's chin now. He shook his head to get them off, but they bit even harder. Both Ferdie and Corny resorted to screaming in pain as the fire ants had their human picnic. Corny couldn't comprehend how such tiny creatures could cause so much pain. The Comanche braves went on eating and watching the fun.

Circling Hawk, standing a good distance away, said, "Skye Fargo the reason you both suffering now."

"Then why don't you feed *him* to the ants?" Ferdie asked, each nip from the ants a new adventure in pain.

"We shoot you now," Circling Hawk said. "Put you out of misery if this would please you. The pain will only get worse."

Circling Hawk barked some orders at his braves. Four of them cocked their rifles, aiming at Ferdie's and Corny's heads.

Judging from the hundreds of venom-laden pinpricks they were laying into the two city slickers, the deadly red ants weren't getting any friendlier. Ferdie felt a battalion of the bastard critters creep under his shorts and bit their way up to his sweetmeats. He tried to decide which was worse—being devoured by thousands of voracious red ants on a flesh-eating frenzy or being gunned down by half a dozen braves with rifles?

Ferdie was reading Corny's mind. Ferdie said, "Which

one do you want, partner, the ants or a bullet right between your eyes?"

"I wish we were at Delmonico's having a couple of juicy, thick steaks and only dreaming about being cowboys," Corny said as a flurry of ants squirmed their way up his chest, ripping and stinging all the way.

"You didn't answer my question," Ferdie said.

"Would you mind terribly if I screamed instead?" Corny asked.

Ferdie and Corny both let out wails of pain that could rouse the spirits of the Comanche dead. Circling Hawk watched impassively as the deadly insects crept their grisly way up the bodies of these stupid white children. Circling Hawk knew they weren't really bad, just ignorant gringos looking to prove their pathetic manhoods, and paying Skye Fargo to help them. Any man deserved to die for being that stupid.

Fargo watched his young employers writhe in agony as the ants treated them like the blue plate special at a cafe. They looked even less happy than when he'd first joined up with them. They were dour then, that first day in San Angelo, but that was only because they had an axe to grind. That was but a mere two days ago, and already they were within hours of being eaten alive.

"You really fixed it this time, Skye Fargo," he said to himself. Had only those boys managed to stay on their horses like he asked, he could have done something. Those boys were dead unless he got himself off the edge of the ridge and went to their rescue. Of course, Circling Hawk was down there, too, just waiting for Fargo to show up. The tortures of the damned would be child's play compared to what that crazy Comanche had in mind for him.

Still, there was really no choice. Fargo knew it. Those boys were his responsibility now, the little peckerheads.

He peered over the top of the ridge. Fargo knew from experience that Circling Hawk sensed his presence. Not too difficult, since he'd blundered into the old Comanche's territory. Despite their ignorance, the boys *were* his friends, and they would be cheerfully fed to the elements if he, Fargo, was too cowardly to rescue them.

Fargo stood behind the ridge. He removed his hat, wiped his brow, then jammed the hat back onto his head.

"To the Devil with you, Circling Hawk," Fargo muttered to nobody in particular.

The Comanche braves continued their lunch and laughed at the two white men as they squirmed in pain. They clearly enjoyed the show.

Ferdie felt the first ant stings on his lips and nose; he was numb from the neck down. Maybe the ants would get full and go away. His screams had given way to pathetic whines, interrupted by promises to God Almighty to never sin again, never touch women or whiskey or ever disobey his father. His cries died hard on the Texas winds; besides, Corny's screams were drowning out his own. Ferdie opened his mouth one last time to beg for a bullet from the Comanche's rifles, and felt ants swinging on his tonsils, making any sounds impossible.

"Ferdie!" Corny bellowed, every inch of his body aflame with ant poison. "If you've got any bright ideas, I'd like to hear them."

Ferdie had none.

Circling Hawk sat with his back to the land behind him, ignoring the screams of the white youths and enjoying the feel of the setting sun on his tawny neck. Then the sun on his back was blocked out, and a shadow fell over him. Circling Hawk breathed deeply and smiled.

"It is you, Skye Fargo," Circling Hawk said, looking up at the hungry buzzards already circling overhead in the vain hope that the ants would leave anything behind.

"You knew I would come," Fargo said.

The braves were well into the cache of stolen white man's whiskey and didn't even hear Fargo approach.

"A hero die many time, a coward only once." Circling Hawk sneered.

"You got it ass backwards," Fargo said, "but dead is dead, no matter how long it takes."

"This true," Circling Hawk responded ignoring Fargo's insult.

"I'm here," Fargo said to the Indian. "Let my friends go."

"Not good enough, Skye Fargo," Circling Hawk said,

watching without emotion as the ants feasted on the *wihios*. "Tell me why I should let them live."

"No," Fargo said. "Tell me why they should die, when it's me you want."

Circling Hawk sat silent for a minute or so, then barked out some orders to his braves. Grudgingly, two of them got up and grabbed sticks of wood from the fire and went to the captives. One brave waved the burning sticks over the two white man and sizzled the ants that were crawling all over them, while the second brave untied the ropes that bound them.

No sooner were the captives freed that they went running, whooping and hollering, slapping every inch of their bodies into the dusk. They both jumped into a small creek in a vain attempt to wash the ants off their bodies, not knowing that the ants couldn't have cared less. The braves watched their misery and roared in laughter. Nothing was funnier than a white man in pain.

Fargo hunkered down next to Circling Hawk and plucked a weed from the brown earth, chewing on it for a spell.

Silence passed between them. Finally, Circling Hawk said, "I much mad at you, Skye Fargo."

Fargo said, "I guess that much."

"Many times we have business together, Skye Fargo," the Indian said. "Why did you choose to deceive me?"

Fargo watched his young friends thrashing about in the creek in a vain attempt to wash the irritating insects off their bodies. The *wihios* could live, but they wouldn't be very pretty for a while. Judging from the screams of his friends, the ants appeared to have other ideas.

Fargo took off his hat, slapped it against the ground a couple of times, and opened his mouth to speak. "Circling Hawk, let me just—"

"I know you well, Skye Fargo," the brave replied. "My heart will tell me if you lie. I will not think kindly if you do."

"The Appleyard brothers ambushed me," Fargo said. "Abel and Clute. Shot me here—" Fargo pounded his left shoulder with his fist "—and left me for dead. Stole every last ounce, the thieving bastards did. Chased 'em all the way to Juarez. Caught up with Clute in a cantina and had to feed him some lead, but by that time I was out of luck.

Abel disappeared down south. Heard he popped up in Tampico, throwing around silver dollars like rain."

"Tell me more," Circling Hawk said.

Fargo did. If he dared lie, Circling Hawk would cut his throat with the bowie knife sheathed on his lap, and then watch as Fargo's life blood spurted into the dry South Texas dirt.

"The day after you gave me the money to buy the whiskey," Fargo said, "Abel Appleyard and me had a few drinks at a saloon in Del Rio. Told him I would pay one silver dollar for every bottle of rotgut he could supply. Went back to the hotel to wait. And damned if he didn't show up at five that morning with fifty-plus cases of the stuff. Told me to bring the money down, two thousand dollars, and it was mine."

Fargo stood and walked over to the fire. He spit into it. He turned to Circling Hawk and said, "If lies were all I had to offer, Hawk, I would not insult you by coming here this very day."

"You return only to save your friends," Circling Hawk said.

"It's mostly my fault they're here," Fargo said. "But they paid me well." Fargo reached into his pocket and pulled out some dusty bills. He handed the wad over to Circling Hawk.

Circling Hawk examined the money. He counted silently. "Five hundred."

"The best I can do at the moment," Fargo said. "I'll get the rest for you somehow."

"The gods of wind and thunder scream at me not to take money, Skye Fargo, but today the sun shines." He pocketed the bills. "Business is business." ·

"I knew you'd see it my way," Fargo said.

"You have new troubles now, the spirits tell me," Circling Hawk said, squatting by the fire. Fargo sat next to him. Ferdie and Corny were still thrashing around in the water. Those red ants played hard, and died even harder. "Bank money from San Angelo," the Indian added.

"Your spirits are wise," Fargo said, and gave Circling Hawk the whole story. The Comanche listened patiently, his dark eyes impassive, giving away nothing as Fargo's yarn unfolded. He was not surprised. This Skye Fargo was an old white man. Honest as most white men went, when they *were* honest, which wasn't often.

"I have heard of this Deke Lonegan," Circling Hawk said. "A very tough hombre. Circling Hawk believe Deke Lonegan will try to cross the border at Del Rio."

"My thoughts exactly," Fargo said. "Will my old friend Circling Hawk and his braves help us?"

The Comanche smiled. "We have been through a lot, my old friend, Fargo," he said. "But as the white man say, 'What in it for me?'"

"The honor of helping an old friend avoid the hangman's noose," Fargo said.

"Then the answer is no," Circling Hawk said. "The army at Fort Stockton wait for Circling Hawk to spill blood and starve our children. I am not coward, but neither am I a fool."

"I understand."

"However," the Indian said, "Circling Hawk buy you drink before you go."

Fargo shrugged. "Why not?"

13

"It's called mescal," Fargo said to Ferdie, handing him a bottle of brownish liquid from his saddlebag, one of six that Circling Hawk had given him that morning upon their departure. "Mex whiskey."

Ferdie took the bottle, and he and Corny examined it.

"What is that floating on the bottom?" Corny asked.

"A worm," Fargo said.

They were trotting along at a slow but steady pace due south. The boys were in their long johns, clothes being too painful to wear. Circling Hawk had supplied them with fresh horses. Their arms and necks and faces were covered with red welts, which the Comanche women had treated with dabs of mud. It dried and sucked out the toxins, but the pain was ever present.

"Should I ask why there's a worm in this bottle?" Ferdie said.

"Best if you don't," Fargo said. "Drink some anyway. It'll cool your pain."

They took turns sampling the mescal, coughing and sputtering. Fargo uncorked a second bottle and took a long drink. The fiery liquid seared his throat and belly. He had no complaints.

As he tried to maneuver his horse through the rocks, thorns, and rattlesnakes, Ferdie said, "How can you be so sure Deke Lonegan and his gang will be holed up in Del Rio?"

"Because there's a steady supply of cheap whiskey and cheaper whores," Fargo said. "And it's spitting distance into Mexico if things get hot. Every dumbshit outlaw figures he's entitled to some rest and relaxation after a job. Lonegan's no different, and Del Rio's the most convenient spot."

"What do we do when we find him?" Corny asked.

"I suspect we'll have to kill him," Fargo said. "If we're lucky."

They rode the rest of the morning in silence. They stopped for a noon dinner under the sparse shade of a live oak. Their main course was jerky, followed by some stale crackers and cold fried rabbit, a gift from Circling Hawk. Fargo declined to share with his friends as he suspiciously thought it might be fried dog. He was saving their meager supply of beans and salt pork for supper. It would be well after noon tomorrow before they'd reach Del Rio. He had to make the necessaries last.

They built a small fire and Fargo put on a pot of weak coffee. Ferdie and Corny ate in silence, looking like they had a bad case of the measles.

Fargo said, "We ought to be hitting Del Rio soon, boys. Things are bound to get rough."

"Every day since we met you has been rough, Mr. Fargo," Corny said. "We've been shot at, chased, beaten by Indians, and left to be devoured by flesh-eating red ants. Don't get us wrong, Mr. Fargo. It's not that we're ungrateful for all the fun you've shown us, but I think it would be best if, when we got to this Del Rio, Ferdie and I wired our fathers for fare back home."

Fargo stared in disbelief at Corny for a second or two, then burst out in an uncontrollable roar of laughter. He laughed long and loud and hearty, enjoying every minute of it, as though he'd been saving it up. There was no joy in it, though. Corny and his friend looked at each other quizzically.

"Go back home?" Fargo snorted. "You think it's all that easy, you dumb peckerwoods?" He was dead serious now. "You got a price on your empty skulls, and I got one on mine. You don't clear your names, and help me clear mine, this robbery is going to follow you every day of your miserable lives, haunting you till the days fall away in misery one by one like the hairs on your heads. Oh, no. We're in this for the long haul. I'm in this because of you two yellow-bellied chunkheads, and we're going to see it through to the last stop on the old trolley car, even if it means layin' gunshot in the street. And if either of you try and run out on me, I'll kill you both, make no mistake."

Fargo poured coffee into a battered tin cup and drank it scalding hot.

The silence was broken by Corny, who said softly, "I thought we were friends, Mr. Fargo."

"We are," Fargo said. "So let's keep it that way." He doused the fire with the dregs of the coffeepot and snapped, "Now mount up."

They did as they were told. It had been less than a week, but both saddled up like they'd been born to it, no falling on their asses or climbing on backwards this time. Fargo smiled to himself. They were learning.

"Now let's get to Del Rio," Fargo announced, and put spurs to flanks. He trotted off at a steady clip through the harsh West Texas terrain.

"His hat must be too tight or somethin'—'cause he's out of his mind."

"I guess," Corny said. "But this is why we came, isn't it? Everything we ever read and dreamed about."

"I know," Ferdie said, shifting his weight to ease the pressure on his tormented skin. "But you know what? Pissing in the middle of Harvard Square never looked better."

They hit Del Rio at midday, an hour later than Fargo had hoped. The boys were in agony from their ant bites throughout the night, and between them both they got maybe forty minutes' sleep. They stopped at a mudhole an hour after dawn so the boys could wallow in it and soothe their burning flesh. They moaned contentedly as if they were getting laid. They were covered with mud from head to toe, looking like a traveling minstrel show.

"Are you certain that Deke Lonegan and his boys are here in Del Rio?" Ferdie asked for what had been the tenth time.

"Like I said," Fargo replied, "it's the most likely place for him to be. Easy passage into Mexico, and enough whorehouses and saloons to keep him and his band of low-lifes happy."

"Are we really gonna kill him if we find him?" Corny asked, scratching at an ant bite on the tip of his nose.

"How the hell do I know?" Fargo said. "I'm making this up as I go along."

"That's very reassuring," Ferdie said.

"Are there any places to eat in this town?" Corny asked, his stomach growling. Del Rio wasn't much as far as towns went; a few saloons, a blacksmith shop, a barbershop, a livery, a run-down hotel and some dusty streets. Mexico was minutes away, across a rickety wooden bridge that spanned the muddy Rio Grande.

"I reckon," Fargo said. "You boys got any money left?"

"You know we don't," Ferdie said. "We're flat broke. What happened to all the money we gave you?"

"Gave it to Circling Hawk in exchange for your lives," Fargo said. This wasn't exactly true, but he owed the Comanche the money and Fargo still aimed to collect for what he'd given to the Indian.

"If you hadn't insisted on going through Indian Territory, you'd still have the money we gave you, and Corny and me wouldn't have been dinner to a million red ants."

"And if I hadn't come back for you two, you'd both be square dancing on air right now. Lucky for you and your bellies, I got my emergency twenty-dollar gold piece tucked away. Should be enough for a meal and a bath. I hate to tell you this, but you're both smellin' kind of ripe."

"What about Deke Lonegan?" Ferdie asked.

"If he's here—and I'm pretty sure he is—he'll keep," Fargo said. "Let's get you clean and fed, and then we'll see to Deke Lonegan."

They were the only customers in the Del Rio Cafe. The locals knew better than to go near the place. For the money, though, they could hardly complain. The food was served by a fat, foul-tempered Mexican woman. Her husband did the cooking, and needless to say the great chefs of Europe had little to fear.

The chili was greasy and didn't have any chunks of meat in it bigger than a baby's fingernail. The little substance to it was of questionable origin. The bread was harder than rock candy, and the coffee tasted like it had been brewed from tobacco. Nonetheless, the trio ate heartily, spooning chili with one hand and swatting the legions of flies with the other. Ferdie picked six fat ones out of the chili, which had fortunately killed the insects on contact.

They had taken baths at the barbershop in cold water; hot water was a luxury they couldn't afford. When they were done eating, Fargo was going to deposit the tinhorns at a ratty hotel down the street, visit some saloons, ask a few questions. He might even have some whiskey. He felt he'd earned it.

"Y'all enjoyin' your supper?" Fargo asked, lighting up a cheroot.

With his mouth full Ferdie said, "One time, a few years ago, I was getting on a train to Boston. There was this old lady ahead of me, ninety if she was a day. She was climbing the steps into the train when it lurched forward. The old lady fell backwards, and her ass landed right on my face. I don't think I've put my lips to anything that bad until I tasted this chili."

"A simple thank you would have been fine," Fargo said.

14

The boys had fallen asleep the minute they'd hit the dirty sheets on the hotel bed. Not even the bedbugs could awaken them. Fargo took the opportunity to see the town.

He was in a charming little spot called the Last Chance Saloon. Fargo chose not to speculate on what the last chance stood for. The place consisted of half a dozen very old tables and chairs in various stages of decay. Exactly the kind of dump Deke Lonegan would feel at home in.

But not today. Except for the greasy, sinister-looking bartender, the joint was empty. "Whiskey, and leave the bottle," Fargo said to him.

The bartender brought the bottle and a dirty shot glass. Fargo flipped a silver dollar onto the bar. The barkeep's hand greedily snatched it up.

Fargo poured himself a drink and downed it. He said to the bartender, "I'm looking for a man, name of Deke Lonegan."

The bartender wiped the scarred surface of the wooden bar with a filthy rag. Without looking up, he said, "Never heard of him."

Fargo flipped another silver dollar onto the bar.

"Think harder," Fargo said. "I happen to know he likes shitholes like this one."

The bartender eyed the silver dollar, not quite sure what to do. That half-second hesitation told Fargo everything he needed to know. He placed a silver dollar next to the first one.

The bartender placed the dirty rag on top of the coins and started to sweep them toward himself. Fargo slapped his hand down on the bartender's.

"You take a man's money, you answer his question first," Fargo said.

"Okay, that's fair," the bartender said. He gave Fargo a steely glare. "I don't know any Deke Lonegan."

Fargo smiled as he grabbed the back of the bartender's head, the greasy hair almost slipping through his fingers. Fargo slammed the man's face hard onto the bar twice until blood was streaming out of his busted nose. The bartender staggered backward into a shelf of bottles. Half of them crashed to the wooden floor and exploded. The bartender held his hands over his face, blood trickling between his fingers.

Fargo took back his two silver dollars. "Sorry, wrong answer," he said, while walking toward the door.

He left without looking back.

Lonegan was either here in Del Rio, or had been recently, of that Fargo was sure. The bartender's silence at the Last Chance Saloon spoke volumes.

Fargo stopped for a drink at two more saloons, the Rotted Molar and The Hitching Post. The bartenders in both places had been about as cooperative as the first, which proved to be not at all, but Fargo had mined a couple of nuggets nonetheless. The bartender at the Rotted Molar had been sullen and silent, but the one at The Hitching Post had stiffened in fear at the mention of Deke Lonegan's name, albeit momentarily. Then conveniently he went deaf and dumb.

There were two or three more dives on the side streets. Fargo sauntered into one of them called the Lilly Mae. The bar was tended by a woman the size of a caboose. She was, Fargo wisely assumed, Lilly Mae her ownself. She stood almost six feet tall and was solid muscle, clad in blue jeans, work boots, and a thick, dirty white cotton shirt. Except for her mammoth breasts, she could have passed for a woodsman.

She was wiping down the bar when Fargo entered. In a voice huskier than gravel she said, "What can I get for you, stranger?"

"Whiskey," he said, trying not to stare at the string of black moustache hairs sprouting on her upper lip. The woman was plain ugly and took no pains to conceal it.

Since it was midday, things were slow. A poker game

was going on at one of the tables. At another, a cute red-head sat sipping a warm beer and playing solitaire. She looked up with some interest when Fargo walked in, then went back to her game.

Lilly Mae poured him a shot. Fargo put a silver dollar on the bar. She went back to her swabbing, stopping to talk to a couple of nattily dressed drummers at the end of the bar. Fargo downed his drink and signaled for another. Lilly Mae dutifully returned and poured him a second. Fargo sipped it.

"Hot one today, ain't it?" he said.

"Seen hotter," Lilly Mae replied.

"Nice town you got here."

"We like it," Lilly Mae said. She sounded bored, polishing glasses with a dirty rag.

"Deke Lonegan been in today?"

Lilly Mae stopped in midpolish, scarcely long enough to be noticeable. Fargo noticed.

"Can't say as I know any Deke Lonegan," Lilly Mae said.

"You sure?" Fargo asked. "He's pretty famous."

"Not around here," Lilly Mae said.

"What if I said I thought you were lying to me," Fargo said.

Lilly Mae polished the shot glass, not looking at Fargo. "Guess I'd have to ask you to be on your way."

Fargo downed the rest of the whiskey. With a wink, he said, "I think you're a lying sack of snakeshit."

Lilly Mae threw her head back and cackled like a wild boar. She grabbed the whiskey bottle and poured him one. "You sure do know how to charm a lady," she said, chortling "This one's on the house."

She expertly flipped the whiskey bottle so she was holding it by the neck, then swung it in the direction of Fargo's head. He pivoted backwards so that she missed by two inches, then grabbed her wrist in midswing. Whiskey poured out onto the bar. Lilly Mae's eyes were red glints of pure hate, her teeth clenched.

With his left hand, he grabbed her nose between his thumb and forefinger, then squeezed and twisted as hard as he could. Lilly Mae howled in pain, dropping the bottle and trying to wrench her nose free with both hands. Fargo held firm.

"Jedadiah!" she wailed.

A giant of a man in the back of the saloon dropped his mop and came charging to his boss's rescue, looking much like a snorting bull. He was even bigger than Lilly Mae, a veritable force to be reckoned with.

Fargo pushed Lilly Mae away and spun to face his attacker. Jedadiah lunged at him. Fargo stepped neatly aside, causing Jedadiah to crash into the bar. Fargo scrambled over to the table where the redheaded bargirl sat and grabbed the chair she was sitting on. He yanked it out from under her and she tumbled to the floor with a grunt.

"You stupid ape," she hissed.

"My apologies, ma'am," Fargo said as Jedadiah's shadow descended on him.

Fargo would swear later that the redhead was smiling. "He's big but his head is made of glass," she informed him.

Fargo didn't hesitate. He swung the chair and smashed it flat against the giant's head, hitting him squarely between the jaw to the top of his skull. The chair broke into several pieces, but served its purpose. Jedadiah looked dazed for a moment, then his eyes rolled back into his sockets, and he collapsed into an untidy heap on the floor.

No sooner was Jedadiah out of the way when Lilly Mae came charging out from behind the bar wielding a huge wooden stick, the better to cave in Fargo's skull. There was black murder in her eyes.

She swung with everything she had, putting her considerable weight behind it. Fargo turned and ducked with less than a second to spare.

Fargo felt himself backing toward the saloon's swinging doors. He ducked as the stick came at him in a savage arc. At exactly that moment, one of the drummers came strolling through the batwing doors. Lily Mae's swing connected with his jaw. The drummer went hurling backward out the doors, out cold even before he crumpled into a heap in the middle of the street.

"Shit on fire," Lilly Mae cackled.

Fargo pivoted back toward the bar before Lilly Mae could turn and bring the wooden stick up for a second try. He grabbed a bottle of rotgut off the bar and smashed it flat into Lilly Mae's ugly face. The bottle disintegrated into sparkly, brown shards, drenching this ox of a woman from head to toe. Fargo waited momentarily for her to react; few men could take a bottle in the face and continue standing. Lily Mae was barely stunned.

She croaked hideously—Fargo thought it might be something akin to a laugh—and came at him, bringing the stick up and aiming straight for anything above his neck. Fargo backed up and found himself pressed up against the bar.

"Teach you to mess with Lilly Mae Cudlipp, you sorry sack of dung," she said almost serenely as she moved in for the kill. Fargo grabbed the butt of his Colt and brought it out of the holster in a flash. Fargo didn't want to kill her, but in that brief moment, both of them knew he would if this progressed.

From out of nowhere, a chair appeared above Lilly Mae, dangling in thin air. Forces unseen brought it crashing down on her head, knocking off three of the legs.

Lilly Mae went down hard, curled up in a ball and ceased to be a problem.

Behind her, still wielding what was left of the chair, was the redheaded bar girl.

She looked down at Lilly Mae, who would be out for the next twelve hours at least and said to no one in particular, "That old bitch's made my life misery from the very day I got to this town."

She dropped the remains of the chair and went behind the bar. She grabbed a bottle of whiskey and poured herself a drink.

"To your health, stranger," she said, and knocked back the rotgut. She poured herself another and said to Fargo, "A simple thank-you might be nice."

"Thank you," Fargo said.

"You're more welcome than you'll ever know," the redhead replied.

She downed the second shot. She poured herself a third, then poured another for Fargo. "You got a name?" she asked.

"Yes," Fargo said.

"Me too," she smiled. They clinked their glasses and drank.

"You had your supper yet?" Fargo took notice of her deliciously long legs.

She swirled the dregs of the whiskey around in the shot glass, not looking at Fargo. "What y'all got in mind?"

"Hot stew, cornbread, and buttermilk," Fargo said.

"I want leg of lamb, potatoes au gratin, and French champagne," she said.

"Okay," Fargo said. "Where do we go to get it?"

"Try the Palmer House in Chicago," she said.

Her name was Miss Olive Elizabeth Chesterfield. She'd been married once to a man named Fenton who was twice her age. This Fenton was an ornery drunk who beat her mercilessly if she so much as burned a bean. Tired of mothering his three slobbering slopeheaded children, she lit out of town with an anvil salesman, who ended up deserting her in Hell's Half Acre down in Fort Worth, Texas. Olive's tale was similar to dozens of others he'd heard from working girls during his many travels.

Olive had more or less worked her way down from Texas to Del Rio over the past year. Six weeks ago, she'd landed here and started to work for Lilly Mae Cudlipp, cadging drinks off drunken cowboys and taking them upstairs for twenty minutes at a time—thirty, if they were of a mind to. Lilly Mae had beaten her and swiped all of her earnings, then knocked her around some more when she complained. Even worse, she confided, when Lilly Mae got drunk she demanded sexual favors from Olive. "Even if she wasn't butt-ugly, I'd have refused," Olive said. "That's not my thing."

Such was the life of a prostitute. Fargo watched Olive devour the thick steak and greasy potatoes ravenously, like the world was ending tomorrow. Her knife and fork were working fast enough to make sparks. They were in a spot called Jenks' Cafe. The food was passable, but it wasn't food Fargo was interested in. As he watched her eat, he sipped a glass of whiskey and lit up a cheap cheroot.

Fargo said to her, "Your employer seemed reluctant to answer my questions."

"Lilly Mae don't much care for questions, I suspect," Olive said. "You done seen that for your ownself."

She snatched another chunk of bread from the basket

and wiped it in the bean juice on her plate. It vanished into her mouth like a fruit bat into a belfry. Her left cheek bulged as she chewed.

She was pretty. Even the hardships of being a frontier whore could not diminish the spark of life in her eyes nor the proud jutting of her wholesome breasts under the tight-fitting, red gingham dress. There was a tired innocence about her that was strangely appealing.

Fargo wanted to take her to bed, and then some.

He sipped some whiskey and said, "What do you know about Deke Lonegan?"

Olive finished chewing, swallowed, and drank some coffee. "This coffee's cold," she said.

"It's better that way," Fargo said.

She continued eating. For a small gal, she did okay in the vittles department.

"Deke Lonegan is in Del Rio," Fargo said, "and I think you know where."

"Would it be too much trouble to get some hot coffee?"

Fargo signaled for the waiter and ordered a pot of hot coffee. When it came, he topped off her cup to heat it up and said, "Happy?"

"Delirious," Olive said. "What y'all got against Deke Lonegan?"

"Enough to bust up most of the saloon owners in this crappy town in order to find him," Fargo said.

She went back to her steak, and said, between mouthfuls, "Can't say as I'm surprised. Slimy little weasel, he is. Never even takes his boots off when he sets to lovin' a woman."

She stared at Fargo, looking somewhat embarrassed.

"So I've been told," she added, looking down at her plate.

"When's he coming back to town?" Fargo asked.

Olive said, "Why should I tell you?"

"'Cause I'm buying you a nice supper," Fargo said. "Also, I'm very nice to women I like. Take my boots off and everything."

Olive speared the last few hunks of fat off the steak and ate them. She said, "You aim to kill him?"

"If need be," Fargo said.

Olive put down her knife and fork. "Got me a nice room," she said. "Sheets are clean, a Mex girl delivers fresh water twice a day. I keep it perfumed and ready to go. If you was to get us a bottle of whiskey, chances are my tongue might just loosen some."

"I'm ready when you are," Fargo said.

Olive looked at him, taking everything in. Her gaze settled on the bulge in his pants. Her cheeks got red.

"Where were you five years ago?" she wanted to know. "When you could've done me some good?"

"Where were you?" Fargo asked.

"Fair enough," Olive said. "Let's get to it."

She stood, and Fargo's heart lurched in his chest. He watched her shapely behind as she walked to the cafe door. "Coming, Mr. Fargo?"

Fargo wiped his mouth with the napkin, though he had eaten nothing, and tossed it over his shoulder.

"I'm coming," he said.

Olive had a small, stuffy room over Crimp's Mercantile. The room consisted of a bed, a bureau, and a small closet. A mild breeze ruffled the dirty, stiff curtains; the late afternoon sun filtered through like mud. Fargo was sweating like a stuck pig but chose not to think about it. The sight of Olive pulling off her dress had his undivided attention.

She wore nothing underneath. Fargo watched her slide between the sheets. She had a farm girl's figure; slim, but with a luscious rear and pouty, cone-shaped breasts. Fargo licked his lips as he glimpsed the dark patch between her legs.

Olive pulled the sheets up to her neck and said, "Y'all lose interest?"

Fargo scrambled out of his clothes and slid into bed beside her. Olive climbed on top of him.

She kissed him, then whispered in his ear, "Treat me right, mister, and I'll treat you right."

"How?" he whispered back.

"Pleasure me good, cowboy, and maybe I'll tell you where to find Deke Lonegan."

Fargo eagerly rose to the occasion. He rolled Olive over onto her back and gazed down at her. Her mounds jiggled invitingly. Fargo took one nipple into his mouth, licking and sucking it tenderly. Olive moaned encouragingly as Fargo switched to the other ruby red nipple, nibbling it playfully. He started kissing and licking his way down the length of her tight little body, burying his head between her legs, where he licked her most intimate spot. Olive writhed sensuously at his touch.

This tall stranger was different from any of the men she'd been with, both for pleasure or otherwise. He actually seemed to care if she had a good time.

He continued lapping at her. Judging from Olive's moans of ecstasy, he was right on target. Women were a lot like horses in many respects; give them a little sugar first and you got a much better ride.

Fargo licked and lapped until she shuddered in orgasmic bliss. He'd made her climax; everything from here on out was strictly gravy. He slid atop her and gripped her tight asscheeks. She willingly spread her legs and wrapped them around his hips. He plunged his stiff rod into her sweet portal and started pumping away.

He jammed his lips onto hers and rammed his tongue halfway down her throat. She made contented moaning sounds, rubbing his sides with the soles of her feet.

He pumped in and out of her with everything he had. They bucked and slithered all over the bed. The topsheet had long been flung onto the floor in their frenzied love-making. Fargo wasn't too sure how long he'd be able to keep from erupting, as Olive had more skillful moves than a New Orleans card shark, one of which involved her middle finger and the sensitive underside of his manhood.

It was a breathless race to the finish. Fargo thought of rocks and trees and droughts, getting kicked by a mule, anything to keep the moment continuing. His efforts were for naught; Olive was just too hot and wet and willing. Her womanly charms were like silk, and twice as smooth.

"Let her rip, cowboy," Olive gasped into his ear, holding him tightly. "You done fulfilled your end of the bargain. Keep on churning till the butter comes."

He was in no position to refuse. He slammed his throbbing member deeply into her one last time and spasmed. Their breathing quickened as a deep shudder wracked his entire body. Olive held on for dear life.

"Sweet Jesus!" Olive cried out.

Spent and sweating, Fargo rolled onto his back and

wiped the moisture from his forehead with the back of his arm.

After resting a few moments, Fargo reached over and grabbed his pants off the floor. He removed a couple of cheroots and lit them, striking a match on the wall behind the bed.

He handed her one. She took it and puffed way. Fargo watched her, naked as a jaybird, the setting sun filtering through the curtains and illuminating her beautiful breasts. Fargo knew he'd want to have another go at her again before the half hour was up, but there was a little business they had to tend to first.

Fargo said, "You promised me some information if I—"

"Yeah, I remember," Olive interrupted. She exhaled smoke. "Why do you want Deke Lonegan?"

"That's my business," Fargo said.

"I'll ask you again: Y'all gonna kill him?"

Fargo said, "And I'll tell you again—if need be."

"That's not good enough," Olive said. "I want him dead, and as quick as possible."

Fargo smoked for a minute, letting that one sink in. "How deep is your grudge against him?"

"Deeper than the deepest part of the Mississippi River," Olive said.

"That's pretty deep," Fargo said. "What did he do to you?"

Olive turned to look at Fargo and said, "There are some things even a whore don't want to talk about, cowboy. This is one of them. Let's just say it was rude, and it hurt a lot."

"All right," Fargo said.

"He and his boys are still here, but I don't know where they're camped," she said. "For a bunch that's wanted by the law, they ain't shy. Come into town every night, drinking and whoring, bragging on how many folks they've killed, throwing money around like it was water."

Fargo shuddered a little. He knew where the money that Deke and his boys were spending like drunken sailors came from. The less cash there was to give back to the bank, the harder it would be to prove their innocence when they did return it.

"Deke took a shine to me," Olive said, the ash on the end of her cheroot growing longer. Her eyes were a bit glassy. "That ain't necessarily a good thing, as I found out. Would've been better off if he'd hated me."

She handed Fargo the slim cigar and rolled onto her belly. Even in the moonlight, Fargo could make out the criss-crossed slashes across her back.

"Jesus," Fargo muttered. "He did that?"

"Deke said I needed to be branded so's I'd be his forever," Olive said. "Man gets hisself a snootful, there ain't no stopping him or his whip."

She snatched the burning Cheroot from Fargo's fingers and took a puff. "Kill him good, Fargo, and you'll never have to worry about getting laid again."

"I'll see what I can do," Fargo said.

"He's here," Fargo said.

Ferdie looked at Corny, who looked back. They both looked groggy. Fargo had gotten them out of bed, and waking them hadn't been easy. They'd been sleeping like dead men.

"Deke Lonegan?" Corny asked. "He's in Del Rio?"

"Just like I knew he would be," Fargo said. He sat in a chair and started pulling his boots off. "Like as not they'll be coming to town tonight to raise some hell."

"If that's true," Corny said, "then why are you getting ready for bed?"

"Because I ain't about to take them on this early when they're full of piss and vinegar," he said, unbuttoning his shirt for the second time that night. "Might be best to try for him at dawn, when he's drunk, red-eyed and slower."

Fargo picked up his boots and made his way to the door. "You best catch some winks while y'all can," he said. "Got us some things to do later. I put myself up in the room next door." He opened the door and stepped out into the hallway. He stuck his head back into the room and added, "Sleep tight, boys."

The door closed. They heard Fargo open the door to the room next door and close it. Footsteps followed, then the creaking of rusty bedsprings as Fargo collapsed onto the bed.

Ferdie and Corny tried to sleep, but it was impossible.

"You scared, partner?" Corny asked his friend in the darkness.

"Right down to my socks," Ferdie replied.

"Me, too," Corny said. "We've never shot it out with outlaws before."

"This is what we wanted, isn't it?" Ferdie asked. "I mean, this is why we came here, right?"

"I thought so," Corny said. "I'm not so sure now. I'm beginning to think it was better when we just read about it."

"There's still time to run," Corny said. "Catch the first train that comes and get on it."

"No," Ferdie said. "For one thing, we have no money. For another, I think I'm more afraid of Skye Fargo than just about anything else in this world."

"This is true," Corny said. "Besides, he *did* save our ham."

"Bacon," Ferdie said. "He saved our bacon."

"Whatever," Corny said.

Neither of them spoke for a few minutes. Then Corny said, "We might die tonight, Ferdie. You ready?"

"Are you?"

"Hell no," Corny said.

"Maybe we won't get killed," Ferdie said. "And if we don't, think of all the stories they'll tell about us. Hell, we can write our own book."

"I don't know," Corny said. "Who would ever believe it?"

"Good point," Ferdie said. "Think you can kill a man if we have to?"

"If it's him or me," Corny said, "the answer is a definite yes."

"Me, too," Ferdie said. "Besides, guns don't argue."

"They don't forgive, either," Corny said.

From the next room, they heard Fargo yell, "Quit jabbering and get some sleep, ladies. Now!"

Ferdie and Corny pulled the ratty blanket up over them, but neither got any sleep to speak of.

15

"You want to get the drop on Deke Lonegan and his boys," Olive had told Fargo, "a couple 'em head straight for the whorehouse the minute they hit town. Ned Thornton and Pee Wee Parker favor two of the gals over at the Purple Tulip."

Fargo remembered this now, and more and more he liked the idea of thinning Deke Lonegan's ranks by two before the real festivities could begin—and by any means necessary—knocking them unconscious or, if need be, killing them. The former was preferable; Fargo hated to kill even when those in question needed killing.

Fargo, Ferdie, and Corny sat at a table in the barroom of the Purple Tulip, playing poker and sharing a bottle of hooch. Fargo was actually trying to teach them the game. For a couple of guys who wanted to be real cowboys, their drinking and card-playing skills were seriously lacking.

Fargo wanted both of them to look as unassuming as possible when and if Lonegan's men came in, so that they would attract as little attention as possible. An honest poker game would arouse the suspicions of few. Also, it served to take his friends' minds off what promised to be an evening of excitement and their last on earth, if things went South.

Fargo looked at Ferdie's cards and said, "Good enough to beat me. You got four of a kind."

"Does that mean I win?" Ferdie asked.

"Depends on what your buddy has," Fargo said.

Corny laid down his hand. He said, "I don't have anything either, except that all my cards came out in order."

Indeed they did. Ten-jack-queen-king-ace.

Fargo said, somewhat angrily, "It's called a straight."

"Does that mean I win?" Corny asked.

"It means you're about the luckiest poker player ever," Fargo said. As Ferdie hauled in the chips—worthless because they were practically broke—Fargo added, "I swear to Jesus, the minute this is over, I'm sending you home even if you have to walk."

"That's over three thousand miles," Ferdie said.

"Yeah," Corny added. Neither of them was feeling much pain. "But it's only fifteen hundred miles apiece."

Ferdie started cackling. He took another drink, but he was still laughing, and whiskey was soon spurting from his nostrils in hilarity.

Corny thought *this* was funny. He started chuckling. But neither of them noticed Bridge and Pee Wee Parker swagger into the saloon and belly up to the bar. Fargo did notice them, however. The other drinkers drifted away from them, giving them a wide berth. Bridge pounded his fist on the bar so hard the shot glasses danced.

"Gimme whiskey," Bridge growled at the bartender, who dutifully placed a bottle and two glasses before them, then wisely made himself scarce at the end of the bar.

Bridge and Pee Wee started sucking up the hooch. Bridge was a barrel-chested brute of a man; Pee Wee Parker was a short, skinny kid, the kind of rotten little toadie who was born to be blasted into eternity before the age of twenty-one. Fargo pegged his age at a year or so less than that.

While Ferdie and Corny attempted to shuffle the deck, succeeding only in spraying cards all over the place, Fargo studied the two men at the bar. If he was any real judge of character, they'd have a few more drinks and then their tempers would demand immediate attention.

Pee Wee knocked back a few and turned his attention to a tall, bony ranch hand minding his own business down at the end of the bar.

"What'd you call me?" Pee Wee barked at the man, who looked up slightly confused.

"You addressin' me, friend?" the ranch hand wanted to know. He showed neither fear nor bravado, only curiosity. He had no idea who he was dealing with, nor did he appear to care.

Pee Wee turned toward him, his gray, beady eyes in tight

little slits. As a tough man, he looked ludicrous. Without Bridge backing him up, even Corny could probably bite his head off.

"Yeah, I'm addressin' y'all," Pee Wee snarled. "You got a problem with that, pig farmer?"

The ranch hand started getting angry. A rusty Colt .44 hung at his hip, but his movements suggested using it wasn't necessary. He put down his drink and faced down the runty little prairie rat who was woefully trying to do the same to him.

"You ain't a nice person," the ranch hand said. "I think you better apologize."

"What if I don't?" Pee Wee asked with a shit-eating grin. Lord, he was a cocky little bastard, Fargo thought.

"I'll be forced to make you," the ranch hand responded.

Even Ferdie and Corny were watching at this point. They both recognized the two men at the bar now, and froze up.

Pee Wee Parker grinned again. Everyone in the joint wanted to slap it off his face, and would have had Bridge not been present. Pee Wee went for his gun, slower than sorghum, his attempts to draw almost pathetic. The ranch hand effortlessly took three giant steps forward and grabbed Pee Wee's arm, twisting it sharply. The pistol never left Pee Wee's holster.

The ranch hand backhanded Pee Wee across the face a couple of times, bringing the little weasel to his knees with ease. He grabbed the collar of Pee Wee's flannel shirt, hoisting him up, then hauled off and popped him flat on the nose, giving the punch everything he had.

Pee Wee reeled backwards and crashed into a table occupied by a couple of drummers, sending mugs of beer and poker chips flying.

"Call me a pig farmer, will ya?" the ranch hand said.

Bridge put his drink down and faced the ranch hand. He said, "That there man you just decked is mah friend."

"What of it?" the man replied. "You want some trouble, too?"

Bridge spit somewhere in the vicinity of the spittoon, his eyes never leaving the formidable rancher. He said, "Nah, I don't want no trouble."

But quick as a striking rattler, he grabbed a fistful of the guy's straw-colored hair and yanked. Before the ranch hand could even react, Bridge drew his pistol, rammed it into the ranchhand's belly, and fired twice.

Even from twenty yards away, Ferdie and Corny watched in horror as the ranch hand clutched his belly, blood spurting between his fingers, the look of shock frozen on his face. Only Bridge's tight grip kept the man from crumpling to the floor.

"No trouble at all," Bridge hissed, pushing the lifeless body away, where it fell into a heap at the end of the bar.

Pee Wee, meanwhile, shakily got to his feet and brushed sawdust from his shirt.

"Fuck with me, will you?" he said to the dead man, giving the corpse a swift kick for good measure. "Guess we gave 'em what for, eh, Bridge?"

"Shut up, you little turd," Bridge said, holstering his pistol. He took another drink, right from the bottle this time. He emptied it and, with a loud belch, hurled it at the mirror behind the bar. The mirror exploded. To no one in particular Bridge said, "Let's get some women."

"Oh, I like women," Pee Wee agreed.

Ignoring him, Bridge made his way up the stairs to the whorehouse and the pleasures that lay beyond. Pee Wee started to follow but not before drawing his gun and threatening everyone in the place.

"Stay cool, you rats," he said. "Me and Al Bridge takes a dim view of showoffs with guns."

He darted up the stairs and vanished down the hallway.

"Killin' that little turd is gonna be a pleasure," Fargo said to his friends.

"Are you going to kill him?" Ferdie asked.

"Only if he begs for it," Fargo said, rising out of his chair. "And I do believe he will."

He made for the staircase. "Stay put. I'll be back," he said to Ferdie and Corny.

Pee Wee Parker spit on the floor. The Mexican whore sat on the bed and watched.

She disliked this scrawny little gringo, who came to her once or twice a week and could only get his rope to rise after slapping her around for ten minutes until she whimpered in pain. His slaps were actually weak and caused her

113

little pain, but for ten dollars in gold coins, she would pretend to be suffering. The little man seemed to enjoy it.

"C'mere, bitch," the little gringo said.

Consuelo went to him, shutting her eyes. She knew what was to follow. She'd seen him humiliated by the tall gringo down in the saloon, saved only by his large amigo, Al Bridge. Now, there was a real man.

When she was facing him—two inches taller than he, even in bare feet—Pee Wee grabbed her cheap dress and whacked her long and hard with the back of his hand.

Consuelo went to her knees, whimpering in mock pain, which excited Pee Wee. He grabbed her black hair and jerked her head back. He slapped her again, with pitiful force behind it. Consuela had gotten ten times as bad from her own father on those nights he came to her, drunk on mescal.

Pee Wee thrust her down onto the bed and began tearing off his shirt, flinging it into a corner and revealing his scrawny, sunken chest. He dropped his blue jeans, then squirmed out of his long underwear. Consuela, eyeing his pathetic little pecker, fought to keep from giggling.

She lay on her back, fully submissive, as Pee Wee climbed on top of her, pinning her shoulders to the mattress. He slipped his little member into her and started pumping for dear life. He grew bored by this in short order, though, and ordered her on her hands and knees. He started pumping her with his swollen needle-dick in and out of her doggie-style, slapping her rear with each thrust until it was beet red.

Fargo, standing outside the door, heard the squeaking bedsprings and the slaps. Pee Wee had started taking his pleasure, such as it was. Al Bridge was happily occupied down the hall in another room with a blond-haired whore. Fargo would deal with him later.

The Mex whore hadn't even bothered to lock the room door. Fargo twisted the doorknob and stepped inside, slamming the door behind him. He stood, leaning against the door, watching Pee Wee pitifully humping the Mex whore, who looked bored shitless.

Pee Wee heard the door slam and looked over at Fargo, annoyed. Twisting his head, he yelped, "Get the hell outta here, bastard."

"My mistake," Fargo said. "Must have the wrong room."

"Your bet your ass you do," Pee Wee snapped. "Get out."

Fargo grinned sheepishly and said, "Well, that presents a problem. See, you're with *my* whore."

Pee Wee's eyes turned wild. Fargo almost relished watching the little hardcase plan his own destruction. Pee Wee said, "*Your* whore? She's mine, you bastard. You better git, or I'll plug you fulla holes."

There were times when life dealt a man four aces with a thousand-dollar stake. This was one of those times, one when an honest man couldn't lose.

"Pee Wee," Fargo said, "you make me feel tired all over when you talk like that."

Still mounted on the Mex whore, though his manhood had shrunk into the size of a grape, Pee Wee said, "How do you know my name?"

Fargo pointed to Pee Wee's deflated manhood. "I didn't," he said. "Your name just seems to match your personality."

Pee Wee scrambled off the bed and made a grab for his holster, which he'd flung onto the floor. Fargo was on him faster than the poor, dead ranch hand had been.

Fargo was in a playful mood. He grabbed Pee Wee by his left ear and gave it a hard yank, almost ripping it from the little bastard's head. Pee Wee opened his mouth to wail in pain when Fargo rammed his fist into Pee Wee's mouth, knocking him into the hardwood floor.

Pee Wee made no effort to get up, instead he glared at Fargo and said, "Who the hell are you, stranger?"

Fargo said, looming hugely over him, "Don't tell me you've forgot already, Pee Wee. The bank in San Angelo? I'm your worst nightmare, but you can call me Fargo."

Pee Wee blinked nervously. He said, "What do you want with me?"

"Nothing," Fargo said. "I just hate men who beat on my favorite whore."

With this, Fargo gave in to temptation and kicked Pee Wee mercilessly until blood was oozing from his nose and mouth and ears. Pee Wee was no longer a problem. Fargo wiped Pee Wee's blood from the tips of his boots with the bedsheet.

"T'ank you, meester," Consuela said when Fargo rose to leave.

Fargo grabbed the doorknob, then said to her, "Was I you, I'd get some better taste in men."

"I theenk, I already do," Consuela said, fluttering her eyes at the tall, handsome stranger.

"Don't tempt me," Fargo said, and turned to leave. This was his first mistake. Pee Wee bounded to his feet, surprisingly agile, and jumped on Fargo's back. He wrapped his scrawny arms around Fargo's neck and tried his damnedest to gouge Fargo's eyes out.

Fargo whirled around, bucking like a bronco, trying to pry Pee Wee's grubby little fingers from his eye sockets. The little rat was stronger than he looked, or at least strong enough to pop Fargo's eyeballs clean out.

For her part, Consuelo remained neutral. Pee Wee was a gringo prick, but he did pay cash money. The other, the tall, handsome *vaquero,* wasn't yet a paying customer, though she hoped he would soon become one. In her business, a girl had to hedge her bets.

Fargo whirled around the room, trying to shake off the much taller man. He backed up against the wall and slammed Pee Wee against it, hard. Pee Wee held on tight, not giving an inch. Fargo repeated the process. Pee Wee was doing a pretty solid job on Fargo's eyes, digging his thumbs into them. Fargo was getting mad.

Consuelo sat on the bed, calmly rolling a smoke for the victor.

Fargo managed to pry Pee Wee's arms from his neck, then grabbed Pee Wee's left wrist and peeled him off his back like a strip of flypaper. He flung the little man onto the bed, crashing into Consuelo.

Pee Wee was up faster than a snake striking a field mouse, this time with a knife. Where he'd been hiding it, Fargo didn't much know or care.

Pee Wee was good with it, too, slashing out at Fargo like lightening. Fargo felt a stinging in the area of the left ear, felt it with his fingers and brought back some blood.

"You little scumsucker," Fargo seethed, in a rage now. Before Pee Wee could slash again with the knife, Fargo slapped it out of his hand in one instant and lifted Pee Wee off the bed. With his other hand he grabbed Pee Wee by the hair, then hoisted the rotten little dwarf up over his head. All sense of reason gone, Fargo hurled Pee Wee at the closed window. Flailing his arms uselessly, Pee Wee sailed through the air for half a second, then crashed through the window with a tremendous explosion of glass and wood, and disappeared from sight with a bloodcurdling scream. Before Fargo could sneeze, he and Consuelo heard Pee Wee's scream cut off abruptly by a sickening thud.

Trying to catch his breath, Fargo said to Consuelo, "Refresh my memory, what floor are we on?"

"The three floor," Conseulo said.

"I was afraid of that," Fargo said, and moved slowly to the ruined window. He looked down. Pee Wee was sprawled in the alley between the saloon and the building next door, atop some now-flattened wooden crates. A bloody slab of wood, Fargo saw on closer inspection, was protruding through his throat. Pee Wee's eyes were wide in lifeless shock. He wouldn't be slapping any more whores from this day on.

Outside, a woman screamed, Fargo heard footsteps on the stairs. The door flew open; standing there was the madam, Miss Aggie March, a blowsy, past-her-prime woman who wore too much make-up to conceal her age. Behind her was a gaggle of whores. Behind them stood Ferdie and Corny.

Aggie looked around, saw the broken window. She said to Fargo, "That window's going to cost you, cowboy. A hundred dollars, to be exact."

"A hundred dollars for a window?" he asked. "That's pretty steep."

"The window's ten," Aggie said. "The undertaker gets the rest."

"Dying sure is expensive in this town," Fargo said.

"I don't doubt Pee Wee needed killing," Aggie said, "but I'd have been grateful if you'd done it somewhere else. I run a clean house."

"Hell," Fargo said. "Just cleaned it for you, didn't I?"

Aggie looked flustered. She said, "We'll discuss this later, mister." She and the rest of her girls started to leave, going downstairs. Ferdie and Corny pushed their way toward the room to have a better look.

Ferdie said, "Did you really throw him out the window?"

"No," Fargo said. "He was just in a hurry."

Ferdie went to the window to have a better look. Corny, standing next to Fargo, asked him, "Is Pee Wee dead?"

Fargo nodded. Down the hall, a door banged out and into the hallway stepped Al Bridge, wearing only his pants and boots. The pistol was clenched in his fist. He fired twice in Fargo's general direction. Fargo heard Corny grunt and topple sideways into him. Fargo caught him and they both fell to the floor. Inside the room, Consuelo screamed and started babbling in Mexican. Pushing Corny away, Fargo scrambled to his feet, cleared leather and fired back, but it was too late—Bridge had dashed down the hallway and down the stairs in a flash. The man could move fast when he had to.

"Corny!" Ferdie cried, going to his friend. Corny's shirt was doused with blood, which blossomed into a big red patch a little below his left shoulder. Corny's face was deathly white.

"Damn," Fargo groused, and knelt to have a closer look.

"Someone's been shot!" Corny said hoarsely.

"You wanna tell him, or should I?" Fargo asked Ferdie.

16

The marshal of Del Rio was named Lattigo Tucker. He was a graying, grizzled, no-nonsense veteran, having kept the peace in half a dozen border towns in Texas and Arizona Territory. He had seen his share of trouble and then some. He tried to rule Del Rio with an iron fist, shooting first and asking questions later, but trying to keep law and order in a town like Del Rio was akin to putting a bandage on a hemorrhage. Judging from the sour expression of his sun-weathered face, Tucker was not at all pleased with some of the recent developments that were transpiring in his town.

He watched as the town sawbones, Doc Dubbins, patched up Corny's arm. Fargo and Ferdie sat nearby. Bridge's bullet had thankfully only grazed Corny.

Tucker hitched his blue jeans up over his considerable gut and said, "I'm well aware that, as of late, Del Rio has been infected by a disease called Deke Lonegan, thank you very much. You still ain't told me why you're a-chasin' him."

"It's for a very good reason I'd like to keep private," Fargo said.

"It ain't private no more," Tucker said. "Not with one man dead and the cathouse all busted up. I got no doubt that fidget needed to die, but tearing up Aggie's place is goin' too far."

It was likely that Tucker owned a piece of Aggie's, hence his appearance here now. Lord only knew, Del Rio was as lawless a town as one could find west of the Mississippi and a routine shoot-out in a whorehouse, while not quite an everyday occurrence, was likely common enough.

Problem was, Fargo preferred not to admit the real reason why he was pursuing Deke Lonegan—that he was after stolen bank money he, Fargo, was accused of stealing. No doubt news of the robbery in San Angelo had reached Del Rio by this time.

"Word around town is," Tucker said, "you got an ax to grind with Deke Lonegan and I want to know why."

Fargo tried to change the subject. He said, "Seems to me, with all Deke Lonegan's wanted for in this territory, you'd have him and his men behind bars by now."

"We don't go looking for trouble in Del Rio," Marshal Tucker said. "It's usually here when we wake up in the morning. Deke Lonegan nor none of his gang have broke any laws here since they arrived. They break the law outside Del Rio, that's no concern of mine. Long as they mind their manners in my town, they're welcome. And Deke's been minding his manners, which is more'n I can say for y'all."

"Does that include Al Bridge putting two bullets in that man's belly in the saloon today?" Fargo asked.

"Self-defense, way I heard it," Tucker said.

Fargo said nothing. There was no point. He drank from a bottle of cheap hooch. After all he'd been through today, he felt he deserved it. Tucker turned his attention to Ferdie.

"You ain't from around these parts," Tucker said to him. "Your features are too soft. I'd guess back East. You got a name?"

Ferdie knew better than to tell this stocky lawman the truth. "Blackheart Pete Newcastle," he said, dredging that colorful moniker from a novel he and Corny had both loved, *Blackheart Pete, Border Ruffian*.

Fargo could do little but roll his eyes in disgust.

"That a fact?" Tucker said. "I seem to remember hearin' old Pete Newcastle took a bullet during a shootout with the Texas Rangers up to Mineral Wells two years ago."

Ferdie hadn't actually finished the book, he now recalled with some panic. He mumbled, "That was a different Blackheart Pete Newcastle."

"Didn't know they was two of 'em," Tucker said. He looked over at Doc Dubbins, who was just finishing bandaging Corny's arm.

"How's our boy doing, Ben?" Tucker said to the doctor.

"It'll be a while before he plays the violin again, but I suspect he'll live," Doc Dubbins said.

"Really?" Corny asked, sounding excited. "You mean I'll be able to play the violin again?"

Doc Dubbins nodded, wrapping the bandage around Corny's shoulder.

"That's great," Corny said. "I could never play one before."

"Where you from, son?" Tucker said, all friendly like.

Before either Fargo or Ferdie could motion for him to keep his mouth shut, Corny said, "New York City, and let me tell you, I can't wait to get back there. I've had enough of the West to last ten lifetimes."

Corny's mouth was off and running. Fargo wanted to empty his pistol into him.

"We came here to have some fun, maybe a little excitement," Corny went on. "We wanted to be desperadoes, you know, just like in all those books we read."

Doc Dubbins had poured some whiskey down Corny's throat earlier to ease the pain, but it also seemed to have loosened his tongue. Corny wouldn't shut up.

"We paid Mr. Fargo good money to help us rob a bank, and you won't believe what happened. We go into the bank in San Angelo—that's where Ferdie and I arrived after we got to Dallas—and we're robbing it when these guys come in and start shooting everybody. I was so scared I almost made chocolate in my pants."

"That a fact?" Tucker asked.

Corny nodded vigorously. "You wouldn't believe what those Indians did to us, either, with the ants and everything. Tell him about Circling Hawk and the ants, Ferdie."

Tucker turned to the other pasty faced tinhorn from back East and said, "Yes, tell me all about it, Ferdie."

Fargo shot Ferdie a look that said, *tell him anything and we're all dead men.*

Ferdie said, "Wasn't anything, really."

"Robbing a bank in San Angelo, runnin' up against Circling Hawk and his passel of murdering red devils," Tucker said. "I would say that's a lot of something."

"Don't pay the boy any mind, Marshal," Fargo said. "He's all delirious from being shot. Can't tell the difference between what he reads and real life."

Tucker ignored him and squinted at Ferdie, giving the young man his meanest flinty eyed look and said, "You know what I think?" He didn't wait for an answer. "I think you're a lying sack of shit. You know what I do to lying sacks of shit in Del Rio?"

Ferdie tried to swallow. His throat was sandpaper.

"I string their skinny asses up in the middle of Main Street and stretch their necks like warm taffy," Tucker thundered. "Then I let their worthless carcasses swing in the summer breeze and get so stinkin' rotten that the flies won't even go near 'em. What do you think about that?"

Ferdie trembled.

Tucker turned to Fargo and said, "You got troubles with Deke Lonegan, you keep 'em out of Del Rio or so help me, as God is my judge and jury, I'll see you all dead."

Tucker made for the door, then turned at the jamb and said, "I do believe I'd be a lot happier if y'all cleared out of town. At dawn. 'Night, Ben."

"Night, Lattigo," Doc Dubbins said.

Tucker slammed the door behind him.

Doc Dubbins finished bandaging up Corny, then started tossing the tools of his trade into his big black bag. He said, "If you men are smart, you'll heed the words of the marshal. That will be five dollars, please."

Fargo managed to hand over three dollars in paper money and whatever pocket change he had, which wasn't much. Doc Dubbins said, with some acid, "Another Diamond Jim Brady. I'll be by tomorrow to change the bandages. Keep him in bed till I get back."

Doc Dubbins left. Ferdie said to Fargo, "Now what?"

"Now what indeed," Fargo said. "Marshal Tucker seemed a little too eager to forgive Al Bridge for killin' a man in cold blood, don't you think? Makes a person wonder why."

"Why?" Ferdie asked.

"It might be in our best interests to find out," Fargo said.

Marshal Lattigo Tucker said to Deke Lonegan, "Who's this Skye Fargo and why's he been tracking you?"

Lonegan said, "Trouble, that's who. Can't believe he's followed us this far. Never thought he'd outrun that posse."

Lonegan and what remained of his gang were camped a mile or so outside Del Rio, by a place called Miller's Creek.

"Yeah, well, he did and now he's here lookin' for y'all," Tucker said. "And I don't think he's a-gonna leave until he gets what he come after. I told you fools to stay out of town until the heat died down, didn't I? Now Pee Wee's dead and folks are startin' to talk."

"Don't get your knickers in a twist, Tucker," Lonegan said, tossing some sticks on the fire. "Where is he now?"

"Over at Aggie's place with his two friends," Tucker said. "But the word is they're broke, so I told her to send 'em packing. Seems Fargo took a shine to a whore in town, girl named Olive. My best guess is, he'll head there."

"Then let's kill 'em and be done with it," Lonegan said.

"Now that's exactly what you ain't a-gonna do," Tucker said. "I don't want no more killin' in Del Rio anytime soon. You boys pack up and head down to the hideout south of the border till you get word from me."

Lonegan thought about it for a minute, then said, "If we can't go to Fargo, maybe there's a way to get him to come to us. Raise the stakes a bit."

"What are you thinkin'?" Tucker asked.

"Go back to the jail," Lonegan said. "Give us a few hours lead time, then head down to the hideout. Odds are you'll lead him right to us. But don't make it easy—that'll tip him off fer sure."

"Okay," Tucker said, rising from the tree stump where he'd been sitting. "Once Fargo and his friends are out of my town, I don't give a fiddler's fuck what you do to him. But you damn well make sure it gets done. Somethin' tells me this Skye Fargo's gonna be one big raspberry seed under my wisdom tooth. Ain't nothing more dangerous in this world than an honest man with a Colt and a Henry rifle."

He started to walk back to his horse. Lonegan said, "Oh, Tucker, I do believe Pee Wee had his bankroll on him when he died."

"That's right, he did," Tucker said. "Over two thousand and change."

"Don't you think you ought to share it with us? We're partners, ain't we? Cut you in all equal-like when we got here."

"That may be true," Tucker said, "but I got the money now, and I'm a-keepin' it. You don't like it, go diddle yourself."

Tucker mounted his horse and trotted off into the night. Lonegan turned to Al Bridge and said, "You know, I think I'll kill him when we don't need him anymore."

17

Fargo said to Aggie March, "I'd be greatly obliged if I could park my friends here tonight. Doc said not to move Mr. Fisk for a spell."

They were sitting in her office in the Purple Tulip, actually a small room off the kitchen. Aggie was all business. She said, "What about that broken window? That's gonna cost you."

"My friends are very wealthy," Fargo said. "Their credit is good."

"I'll be the judge of that," Aggie said, pouring herself a drink. She offered Fargo one, which he gratefully accepted.

Things didn't smell quite right in Del Rio—Marshal Lattigo Tucker, for his part, was a little too eager to see Fargo and his pals ride on out of town, not to mention his reluctance to discuss Deke Lonegan and his gang in any detail. Also, there had to have been a bounty put on Fargo's head by this time for the robbery in San Angelo, in which Tucker seemed not the least bit interested.

Miss Aggie March might very well hold the key to this little mystery.

Fargo said, "Quite a marshal you have here in Del Rio. Not sure I like him."

"Lattigo's just doing his job," Aggie said, a little defensively. "It's not easy keeping law and order in a border town like this."

"No, I guess not," Fargo said. "Would you say he's an honest man?"

"As honest as you'll find in this part of the world," Aggie said. "Why do you ask?"

Fargo shrugged. He said, "You sleeping with him?"

Aggie didn't flinch. She was a cool one. She said, "What interest is that of yours, Mr. Fargo?"

"Well," Fargo said, "I'm assuming you two are partners in this place. I was just wondering if that carried over into the bedroom."

"You son of a whore," Aggie said, opening a drawer in her desk. She pulled out a nice little pearl-handled revolver, which she pointed at Fargo's belly—exactly the response he was hoping for.

She stood, still pointing the revolver. Fargo rose to his feet wearily. It had been a long day, and it wasn't done yet.

She said, "I think this conversation is over, Mr. Fargo. You ask too many questions, and that can make things real prickly in this town. I want you and your friends out of here now, tonight. And if you got even a little brain in your head, you'll take Tucker's advice and make your own-selves real scarce."

"Funny," Fargo said. "You're the second person tonight who's made that suggestion."

He turned to leave, then whirled around and in one little deft motion, grabbed the revolver out of Aggie's hand and gave her a healthy shove backwards into her chair.

"You rotten son of a whore," she hissed.

"You know," Fargo said, emptying the chamber of bullets and tossing the gun onto the desk, "you're beautiful when you're angry."

Fargo heard a vase hit the door and shatter as he closed it behind him.

Olive opened the door to her room and saw Fargo and two strange looking men with him. They were both younger than Fargo, tinhorns both, pale-faced and skinny. The one in the middle—the one Fargo and his friend were holding up—was looking a little green around the gills.

"Skye?" Olive said.

"Hello, Olive," Fargo said, and then he and his friend dragged the one in the middle into her room.

"Staying the night, are you?" Olive wanted to know, watching as Fargo and his friend dumped the third one onto the bed, where he curled into a little ball.

Fargo said, "If that's okay with you."

The young man on her bed started snoring immediately.

Olive couldn't help but see the gunshot wound on Corny's shoulder. "He doesn't look so good," she said.

"He'll be fine, with some of your very own loving-tender care," Fargo said.

"Are you in trouble, Fargo?" Olive asked.

"What do you think?"

"You're in trouble," she concluded. She said, motioning to Corny, "What am I supposed to do with him?"

"Just keep him out of sight, whatever you do, until I get back," Fargo said.

"And if you don't come back?" she asked.

"Then he's all yours," Fargo said. "And you could do worse—he's got a very rich daddy." He turned to Ferdie and said, "Let's get moving, chunkhead."

"Where are we going?" Ferdie asked.

"Straight to hell, son," Fargo said. "Straight to hell. Although, you may know it as Mexico."

When they were gone, Olive sat on the edge of the bed where Corny was drifting in and out of a restless sleep. She dipped a towel into some cold water and wiped his brow with it. The poor boy was as white as a sheet; he'd obviously lost more blood than he could afford to.

He slept for an hour or so, then woke up. Some of his color had returned, but he was a little weak. "Where am I?" he asked Olive.

"My place," she said. "My name is Olive, I'm a friend of Mr. Fargo's. What's your name?"

"I'm Cornelius, though my friends call me Corny," he said. "Where's Fargo? Where's Ferdie?"

"Your friends went to take care of some business," she said. "Skye asked me to keep an eye on you, and that's what I aim to do."

Corny bolted from the bed, saying, "I've got to find them. They need me. Deke Lonegan—"

Olive eased him gently back down onto the pillow, and said, "You ain't going anywhere, hombre. They'll be back. Fargo knows how to handle himself, so stop worrying. Are you hungry?"

Corny nodded and said, "Yes, I guess I am."

Olive went down to the cafe and returned with a big fat ham sandwich, a huge slab of apple pie, and a cold glass of lemonade, all of which Corny devoured. He started feeling much better.

He asked Olive, "How do you know Mr. Fargo?"

"We're business associates," she replied, sitting on the edge of the bed as he ate. "Your daddy really rich?"

Corny swallowed and said, "Yes. He expects me to go to work for him when Ferdie and I go home—if we ever do get to go home, that is." He proceeded to pour his heart out, describing the whole ball of wax to her, starting from the day they boarded the train in New York. He rummaged through his saddlebags and pulled out a battered notebook.

"I've been keeping a diary since the day we left," he said blushing. "Because, the thing is, I don't really want to work for my father."

"No?" she asked.

He shook his head. "I want to write dime novels, like the ones Ferdie and I read. I want to write about our experiences here in Texas. I've already got the title: *Bullets Don't Argue.*"

"I'd like to read it when you're done," Olive said. "Or I would, if I knew how to read."

"Maybe I could read it to you," Corny said, noticing now how pretty she was. He found himself staring at her tits until she caught him in the act. He blushed again.

She asked him, "Have you ever been with a woman before?"

"Well," he replied. "Fargo took us to a place in San Angelo where the women—"

"Nellie's place?" she asked.

"That's right," he said, and described his less than satisfying encounter with Lulubelle. Olive responded with, "You need a real woman."

"You're probably right," Corny said. "Do you know any?"

"I might," Olive replied, and started undressing. She dimmed the lamplight to a bare minimum and climbed onto the bed. She sat facing him and asked, "Do you like what you see?"

It was hard not to. He nodded vigorously. She said, "Let's take off some of those clothes and get you more comfortable."

She helped him pull off his pants, and then she unbuttoned his shirt. Even in the dim light of her room, she noticed the little red welts all over his chest. She said, "What in the name of Jesus happened to you?"

"Ferdie and I were attacked by some red ants," he said. "It hurt something fierce."

She kissed his chest and neck, making it all better. Corny's manhood started rising to the occasion. She whispered in his ear, "Would you like to touch my titties?"

"I'd be crazy not to," he said. Olive gently took his hands and placed them on her plump, mouth-watering mounds. He said, "What do we do now?"

"I think you know the answer to that," she said. She took him in her arms, pressing her breasts lovingly against his chest, and kissed him deeply. Corny didn't know exactly what to do with his hands until she said, "Take off your undershirt, baby."

He tried pulling the undershirt off over his head, where it got hung up on his ears. He started wrestling with the stubborn, dirty undergarment, getting more and more frustrated. Olive went to offer her help just as Corny was raising his left arm, hitting his square on the chin with his elbow. She tumbled backward off the bed and flopped to the floor, and thank the Lord she'd put down a nice rug there a week earlier.

Corny managed to yank the cursed shirt off his head. Olive was gone. He wondered if he'd dreamed her. "Olive?" He crawled over to the right side of the bed and looked down, with no success. He crawled over to the other side of the bed, peered over, and got Olive's fist on his chin.

He said, shaking his head, "What did you do that for?"

"Dumbbell," she snapped. She grabbed him by the hair and pulled him off the bed, where he landed flat on top of her. Olive wasted no time, and grabbed his stiff member and eased it into her warm wetness. Corny did what came naturally, going at her with the awkward enthusiasm of youth. His strong, steady thrusts into her were met with equal passion from Olive, and they were quickly bouncing all over the floor. Their heated thrashings continued with hungry abandon until they were inches from the wall.

"Oh, do me, lover, do me," Olive gasped, spreading her legs wider. Corny lifted himself up, palms flat on the floor, and pumped her even more furiously. They slid back even

129

further toward the wall; Olive's head started thumping against it as Corny went at her, deliriously oblivious to her plight.

He spasmed inside her, having never known anything could feel so pleasurable. His eyes crossed and his breath coming in ragged gasps. When his climax subsided, he collapsed on top of her, totally exhausted and unaware that Olive was out cold.

Still on top of her, he said, "That was very nice, Olive." When he got no response, he said, "Did you have a nice time, too?"

He was greeted with silence. He looked at her; her eyes were closed. "Olive?"

She'd fallen asleep on him while he was making love to her! Corny was angry, ashamed, insulted, and felt another dozen emotions, none of them good.

He said, "I may not be as good as Ferdie when it comes to doing it, but I have to say, Olive, I'm very hurt. Was it that bad?"

More silence. With panic rising in his voice, he said, "Olive? Are you all right? Olive? Say a few syllables."

Panic set in. He gently slapped her face, but she was down for the count.

At that very moment, the door to her room was kicked open, shards of wood flying everywhere, and in barged two mean-looking men. One of them was Chinese, like the ones who did the laundry back home, but the strangest looking Oriental Corny had ever seen. The other one was tall and stocky, and looked like he hadn't shaved in a week. Corny felt like he had seen them before, but couldn't quite remember where or when.

Al Bridge pointed to Corny and said to Flat-Eye, "That's one of 'em."

Together they grabbed Corny, who was still naked as a jaybird, by the arms and tossed him onto the bed.

Corny said, "Were we making too much noise?"

Bridge and Flat-Eye looked down at Olive, who was still unconscious. Flat-Eye grinned and said, "They do fucky-fucky on floor."

"So it appears," Bridge responded. "What'd you do, son, screw her to death?"

"I didn't mean to kill her," Corny said, on the verge of tears. "It was an accident, really. We were just—"

Bridge plucked Corny's pants off the floor and threw them in Corny's face. "Put your britches on, son. There's someone wants to meet you."

"She's not really dead, is she?" Corny said, close to hysteria now. "I'm in enough trouble as it is. I don't want—"

Al Bridge motioned to the small Chinese guy. Flat-Eye brandished a very long knife and held it at Corny's throat.

"I said," Bridge repeated, "get dressed." He meant business.

"Am I under arrest?" Corny asked, carefully pulling on his pants, his gaze never leaving the knife at his throat. Not surprisingly, he put his pants on backwards.

"Son," Bridge replied, "you're gonna wish you were when Deke Lonegan gets through with you." Bridge descended on Corny, whacking him on the skull with the butt of his pistol. The inside of Corny's head became the Fourth of July, complete with fireworks and bottle rockets.

Fargo and Ferdie stood stock still by the side of Dilbeck's Dry Goods Store, shrouded in darkness. Their horses were behind them. Across the street was the Del Rio jailhouse. Fargo never took his eyes off it. Though it was four in the morning, there was still a fair amount of people on the streets: Mexicans, drunken cowboys looking for whorehouses, gamblers, and the like. Border towns never sleep, Fargo told Ferdie.

"What exactly are we watching for?" Ferdie asked for the third time.

Fargo said, "The esteemed Marshal Lattigo Tucker, if my figurin' is correct, is going to lead us straight to Deke Lonegan."

Not two minutes later, Tucker left the jail and saddled up his horse. He mounted up, put spurs to flanks, and rode off briskly.

Fargo said, "Time to move."

They mounted up quickly and followed Tucker, though at a safe distance. As Fargo had predicted, Tucker headed straight for the bridge over the Rio Grande into Cuidad Acuna, on the Mexican side.

As they crossed the bridge into Mexico, Fargo said to

Ferdie, "We're about to pass through the gates of Hell, son. Whatever you do, don't talk to anyone, don't answer if they talk to you, and always, *always* look straight ahead. Mind your p's and q's, Ferdinand, and that's an order."

Fargo was on the money. If Del Rio was bad, Cuidad Acuna was worse—as though the dregs of humanity, plopped down from the four corners of the earth, had landed in this dusty, dirty town. Ferdie had never seen so many greasy, scarred up faces, so many missing eyes and ears and, in some cases, fingers or even entire arms.

"We're going to die tonight, aren't we?" Ferdie asked.

"That's a possibility," Fargo said.

From the corner of his eye, Ferdie saw a group of hard-looking men armed to the teeth with bullet belts criss-crossing their burly chests, standing in front of a cantina. They stared with pure hatred at the *gringos Americanos* as they passed.

"Why are those men staring at us?" Ferdie asked, looking straight ahead. He could feel those hostile gazes burning against his back. "They look angry."

"Angry?" Fargo replied. "Hell, boy, those are bandits. Murderin' devils, the lot of 'em. They'll cut your heart out for the pennies in your pocket."

"My heart?" Ferdie asked. "That's my second favorite organ."

Cuidad Acuna was a world away from Gramercy Park. Dogs and pigs and chickens and goats roamed freely; little brown naked children scurried in the streets. Most of the structures were made of what looked like mud, low to the ground and in various stages of decay. Here and there were wooden structures, mostly cantinas and ramshackle hotels with cockroaches so big they could push a grown man out of bed. At one cantina, a drunken free-for-all spilled out into the street—a dozen mad Mexicans, blasted on mescal, savagely slashing at each other with knives. Even the whores joined in on the fun, eye-gouging, hair-pulling, and crotch-kicking. A gaggle of nasty little children squealed delightedly at the spectacle, throwing manure—some dry, some wet—on the brawlers.

Fargo and Ferdie rode by in stone-faced silence. Lattigo Tucker had long since melted into the night, and Ferdie was tempted to suggest they speed up a bit. He wisely held his tongue; he'd learned to trust Fargo's instincts.

As if reading his mind, Fargo said, "If Tucker's smart, he'll know he's bein' followed. We just take it slow and steady."

They rode on, coming to yet another noisy cantina. Fargo brought the Ovaro to a halt.

"What is it?" Ferdie asked.

Fargo pointed to the hitching post. Tucker's horse was tied to it.

"Strange time to stop for a drink," Fargo said, and dismounted.

"Where are you going?" Ferdie asked.

"It's not where am *I* going, it's where *we're* going," Fargo said. "And where *we're* going is in there."

From where he sat, Ferdie looked inside the cantina. What he saw were lots of mean looking hombres.

Ferdie asked, his eyes wide in terror, "Couldn't I just wait here?"

Fargo grabbed Ferdie by the leg and pulled him hard off the horse. Ferdie tumbled onto the street with a grunt.

"What the hell did you want that for?" he asked indignantly.

Fargo yanked him to his feet and said, "You came west for adventure, kid, and that's just what you're gonna get."

Fargo pulled the Henry from the scabbard and strode confidently into the cantina, Ferdie followed nervously at his heels like a frightened puppy. They were greeted with two dozen of the most savagely sinister hardcases Ferdie had ever seen, faces he knew would haunt his dreams for years to come. There wasn't a full set of teeth in the entire place, and the rancid, sour odor of sweat, tobacco, and cheap tequila was overpowering. Ferdie fought the urge to go screaming out into the night and followed Fargo to the bar. If the tall man was scared, he was doing an excellent job of hiding it.

The place fell silent, all eyes upon them.

"Tequila," Fargo said to the bartender, who was fat, sweaty, and unshaven. He wore a filthy apron that might have once passed for white. Fargo looked straight ahead, ignoring the hostile glares. Ferdie looked straight ahead, too.

Ferdie said, "He's not here."

"Yes, I can see that," Fargo said. "That son of a whore Tucker tricked us."

The bartender slapped a bottle of tequila on the bar, along with two glasses he proceeded to clean with the filthy rag. He poured them each a shot. The thought of drinking it turned Ferdie's stomach. The bartender looked at them sternly, waiting.

"How are we going to pay for this?" Ferdie whispered.

"Haven't thought that far ahead," Fargo said. He sipped some tequila and said to the bartender. *"Donde esta Señor Lattigo Tucker?"*

The bartender stared at him mutely, shrugged, and shook his head. He said, in Spanish, "I do not know any Lattigo Tucker."

A group of skinny desperadoes, their faces streaked with dirt, approached Fargo and Ferdie. The desperadoes were armed to the teeth, and looking for trouble. Ferdie craned his neck slightly to get a better look.

"They're coming this way," Ferdie said.

"Stay cool, kid," Fargo said. "These devils can smell fear."

"If fear smells anything like this place, we're dead men."

The hombres, about six of them, surrounded Fargo and Ferdie. One of them plucked Ferdie's hat off his head and examined it, obviously liking what he saw. He replaced the ratty old hat he'd been wearing with Ferdie's, and it was clear that he had no intention of giving it back.

"Now what?" Ferdie said to Fargo.

"Do what you have to do," he replied. "Show 'em you ain't afraid of 'em."

"And how do I accomplish that?" Ferdie asked.

"Take your hat away from him," Fargo said, "and pray."

Ferdie did just that, placing his hat firmly back on his head. "My hat," he said, pointing at his head and wishing he knew how to speak Mexican. Instead, he groped in his mind for any words in a language other than English. *"Capiche?"* he added in Italian, hoping it was close enough.

The Mexican tried to go for Ferdie's hat again. Ferdie grabbed his wrist and gave it a twist. The Mexican backed off and came back with a pig-sticker, murder in his lifeless black orbs. He intended to carve his initials on Ferdie's face.

His compadres backed off, leaving the field clear for the fight. One Mexican near Fargo whipped out his knife and attempted to help his friend. Fargo gave him a hard chop to the throat, dropping him on the spot. The Mexican went for his gun; Fargo neatly knocked it out of his hand with his boot and stomped on the guy's head, saying, "One at a time, here, *señor*."

Ferdie, meanwhile, held his ground against the Mex with the knife, who slashed wildly in Ferdie's general direction. Ferdie jumped back, and the Mexican moved in again, the knife glinting in the dim light of the cantina. Ferdie never even felt the metal cut his flesh, only saw the patch of red spread on his shirt. The Mexicans in the joint started cheering approvingly.

"You greasy piece of slime," Ferdie muttered, angry now. Since arriving in Texas, he'd been shot at, chased by a posse, attacked by Indians, devoured by ants, and now cut by a weaselly little Mexican. Enough was enough.

The Mexican slashed at him again. Ferdie jumped backwards, next to Fargo, and said, "Feel free to jump in any time," as the skinny Mex lunged at him again.

Ferdie dodged him, hearing Fargo say, "You're doing fine, kid," and remembered a scene he'd once read in *Black Ear Cicero, Scourge of Colorado Territory*. He grabbed a tequila bottle and smashed it against the bar, thinking he'd cut the Mexican back with the jagged bottleneck. Unfortunately, the bottle disintegrated into a thousand little pieces, leaving only two inches of brown glass in his hand. The Mexicans roared with laughter. Ferdie had never felt so humiliated.

The Mexican cut him again, this time on the left wrist. Ferdie backed away. Without breaking a sweat, the Mexican charged at him. Ferdie took one step backwards and tripped him up. The Mex went flying into the bar and bounced off, dropping the knife. Before he could regain his balance, Ferdie landed a perfect haymaker with everything he had on the Mex's chin. The Mexican went down hard but not for long—he went for his *pistola*. Ferdie drew his Colt and fired, hitting the man in the throat. Blood spurted up like a geyser—Ferdie had never seen so much blood. At the same time, two of his buddies drew their *pistolas* to even up the score. They weren't quite fast enough, however; Fargo plugged them both, one right in the forehead, the other right below the left eye. They ceased to be a problem.

Between them, Fargo and Ferdie discouraged further heroism on the part of the remainder of the patrons. Fargo turned to the bartender, jammed the barrel of his Colt squarely on the fat man's nose, and said, "I'll ask you again: where the hell is Lattigo Tucker?"

The bartender swallowed hard and replied, "He come in before, *señor,* but then he leave and I not know where he go."

Fargo cocked the trigger and said, "I'll ask you again—where is he?"

The bartender stammered, "Calle San Carlos, south of here."

"Better." He holstered the colt. He said to Ferdie, who was staring at the dead Mexicans as though in a dream, "We best be on our way." When Ferdie didn't immediately respond, Fargo grabbed him by the arm and escorted him out, grabbing the bottle of tequila with his other hand.

When they were gone, the bartender said, "Thees job is getting too dangerous for me."

18

"I helped kill that man," Ferdie said, his voice sounding a million miles away.

"It was him or you, son," Fargo said, cleansing Ferdie's wounds with tequila. "You did what you had to do." They were on the southern outskirts of Cuidad Acuna, deeper into Mexico than Fargo would have liked. It was a cloudless, starry night, and hotter than any August in West Texas that Fargo could remember. He kept a wary eye on their surroundings, just in case some of the dead Mexicans' friends decided to pay a visit.

"I still can't believe I helped to kill someone," Ferdie said. "It just doesn't seem real."

Ferdie was still in shock, and would be for a spell. Killing your first human being would do that. Fargo set to bandaging Ferdie's cuts, some of which were deep. He made Ferdie drink some of the tequila, then made him drink a little more.

Fargo said, "If it helps any, Ferdinand, you handled yourself real nice back there. You ought to be proud of that. And as for killin', well, you may yet be doing more before this is all over. So you best get used to the idea."

Ferdie said, "Would it be okay if I went to sleep for awhile?"

Fargo said, "No, it wouldn't. We got things to do."

"Thank you," Ferdie said ignoring him. "I think I'd like to become unconscious now."

He closed his eyes and went out like a light, starting to snore contentedly. Fargo sighed. Tinhorns. They'd be the death of him yet.

There was a small creek nearby with barely enough water flowing through it to drown a crawfish. Fargo took Ferdie by the scuff and dragged him over to it, then jammed his head into the few inches of water. "I mean for you to relax, not go south on me," he said.

Ferdie breathed in the rancid water. He opened his eyes, coughing and spitting water out through his nose, then went back to sleep again. Fargo gave him some hard slaps across both sides of his face.

"Wake up," Fargo barked. "I told you, we got things to do."

Ferdie's eyes fluttered open. He grinned like a dope and said, to Fargo, "Tell me a bedtime story, Mama."

"A bedtime story," Fargo grumbled, and gave Ferdie another dunking. Fargo stuck his own head into the creek and sucked down as much water as his belly would allow, he was thirsty. He drank his fill, then gave Ferdie another dunk and slapped him more until he came around. "Once upon a time," Fargo started, "there was a dumbass little brat from New York who died a violent death because he wouldn't get right with himself when the going got tough."

He got Ferdie to his feet and managed to prop him up on his horse, but not without some difficulty. Ferdie listed to the left, slipping out of the saddle, and Fargo tried three times to prop him up. Satisfied that he would stay put for the next few minutes, Fargo mounted his Ovaro and started riding south, hoping for the best. He rode a few yards, then looked back. Ferdie was astride the horse but that was all. His head hung on his chest.

Fargo went back and grabbed the reins of Ferdie's horse. Leading the kid deeper into the Mexican night, Fargo said, "They ain't paying me nearly enough for this."

Three hours later, a little before dawn, they crested a brown, dusty hill. On the other side was a small, tired-looking, sparsely populated town—San Carlos, no doubt. Bone-thin, flea-bitten dogs outnumbered people four to one. San Carlos consisted of a church, a cantina, and a scattering of poorly constructed shacks. Not exactly heaven on earth, but an excellent location for a bandit hideout.

Ferdie had come around, more or less, the shock finally wearing off. He would not be returning home the same young, innocent man he'd been. They stopped to give the horses some grain and rest.

Ferdie looked down at the small town from where they'd

stopped on the top of the hill, observing, "This place makes even Acuna look like paradise."

"No," Fargo said, "but if you're looking for a place to disappear, it's perfect."

They rode on into town, stopping—no surprise to Ferdie—at the cantina, where a dim light burned in the small window. The place was deserted except for one Mexican man who snored on top of the bar, which was actually several wooden planks resting on barrels.

Fargo woke him up. "Tequila?" the man asked.

Fargo shook his head, and started talking to the man in Spanish. The man responded here and there with a one- or two-word reply. Fargo thanked him, and the man curled up on the bar and went back to sleep.

"A cabin, about a quarter-mile south of here," Fargo said. They mounted up and trotted away.

"Something just ain't right with this picture," Fargo said.

They were looking down on the cabin. It was nestled under a rocky ridge amidst clumps of mesquite, making any assault from the rear of the structure impossible. There were no side windows that he could see, which was a plus. A thin tendril of smoke rose from the chimney. Fargo counted four horses, including Tucker's. If they were expecting company down there, and Fargo was pretty certain they were, they didn't seem too concerned about it. That troubled him. There was the possibility that Tucker, by leading them into that cantina, had never expected them to leave there alive. Fargo wasn't quite satisfied with that scenario, though.

"Seems quiet down there," Ferdie said.

"Yeah, too damn quiet," Fargo said.

"Maybe they're asleep," Ferdie suggested.

"I wouldn't count on it."

Fargo considered setting the cabin on fire if he could get close enough to the right side of the structure. It was risky and no mistake; there was an excellent chance he'd get gunned down before he could even get close, which would defeat the purpose. Before Fargo could even decide on a plan of action, however, the door to the cabin opened. Corny, trussed up like a Christmas goose, was pushed outside, where he fell face down into the dirt. He was followed out by Deke Lonegan and Al Bridge.

"Oh, my God," Ferdie cried in horror. "It's Corny."

"What the hell is he doing here?" Fargo growled.

Lonegan threw a rope over a low branch of a live oak tree, while Al Bridge hoisted Corny across the saddle of a horse, yelling at him to sit up straight. Bridge took the horse's reins and led him over to the live oak. Lonegan tied one end of the rope into a hangman's noose, which was promptly placed over Corny's head.

"They're going to hang him!" Ferdie said, his voice verging on panic. "We've got to stop them, Mr. Fargo. He's my best friend in the whole world. We can't—"

"I know you're out there somewhere, Fargo!" Lonegan called out. "Let's finish this. Come out with your hands in the sky, real slow like, and bring your buddy with you. Any tricks and your friend here is a dead man."

Fargo started to stand. Ferdie grabbed his arm. He said, "You're not really going down there, are you?"

"Your friend's life may depend on it," Fargo said. "Give me your gun."

Ferdie handed Fargo his Colt, which Fargo tucked neatly under his belt against the small of his back. He said, "Whatever you see, whatever you hear, don't move from this spot." He pulled the Henry from the scabbard and handed it to Ferdie.

"Ever use one of these?" he asked.

Ferdie said, "Why would I?"

"That's what I thought," Fargo said. "When the shit starts flying, shoot at anything that ain't me."

Fargo raised his hands and made his way down the ridge toward the cabin. Corny, sitting on the horse, saw him coming and brightened visibly. As Fargo approached the cabin, Lonegan cocked his rifle and aimed it at him. Lonegan said, "That's close enough, mister. Drop that gun belt, and do it real slow."

Fargo stopped and did as he was told. When he was done, he raised his arms up again, without being told.

Lonegan said, "Where's your friend, mister?"

"Dead," Fargo said. "Took a bullet in that lovely cantina Mr. Tucker lured us into. Ain't no big deal."

Corny did not take this news well. Though he tried to

hold them back, tears leaked from his eyes and his throat got all tight.

"He's lyin'," Tucker said. "I know he is."

"Then you won't mind if we kill this other one," Lonegan said, ready to slap the horse's butt and leave Corny hanging in the breeze.

"I didn't mean to kill Olive, Mr. Fargo," Corny pleaded. "Really I didn't. Mr. Bridge said I screwed her to death. Is that possible?"

"Shut up, you sorry bastard," Lonegan hissed at Corny.

"Ain't no skin off my nose," Fargo said. "Hang him if you're of a mind to."

Lonegan said to Fargo, "Why you been trackin' me, big man? What did I ever do to y'all?"

"You robbed a bank in San Angelo and killed some people," Fargo said. "I got the blame. I aim to get the money back and clear my name."

Lonegan chuckled and said, "Ain't much chance of that happenin', mister."

"Sweet limpin' Jesus, Lonegan," Tucker cried. "What the hell you waitin' for? Kill him and let's be done with it."

Lonegan turned to Tucker and said, "You know, Lattigo, you really get on my nerves." He shot him twice in the face. Tucker went flying backwards and dropped, dying where he fell.

Fargo seized the opportunity. He reached behind, under his belt, and pulled out Ferdie's Colt. He fired once at Lonegan and missed, then dropped to the ground and rolled behind a good-sized chunk of rock jutting out of the ground. It wasn't much in the way of cover, but he wasn't being picky. Lonegan made it behind the live oak, and squeezed off two shots, kicking up rocks and dust into Fargo's eyes. The gunshots frightened Corny's horse, which bolted off to parts unknown. Corny started dancing on air, kicking his legs and clawing wildly at the rope as it cut into his neck. Inside the cabin, Bridge started firing at Fargo as well, making things much more uncomfortable.

Up on the ridge, Ferdie sprung into action, fumbling with the Henry—the damn thing weighed a ton—and aimed at the cabin window. He fired, unprepared for the Henry's kickback, which knocked him flat on his ass and stunned him momentarily. He shook his head to clear it, and when he refocused his eyes, a deranged looking Chinese guy was standing over him, cocking a pistol.

The Chinaman giggled like a lunatic and said, "You fucky-fucky?"

"No," Ferdie said. "Ferdinand Bertam Wallingford the Second, from New York."

Ferdie struck like a Gila monster, leaping at Flat-Eye's ankles. The Chinaman was too quick, squeezing off a shot into the calf of Ferdie's leg before Ferdie tackled him to the ground. Ferdie was all over him, pummeling Flat-Eye with his fists. He had yet to feel the pain of the bullet, but he did feel the searing, red-hot pain in his left side as the Chinaman stabbed him. Ferdie saw the glint of a bloody knife as Flat-Eye tried to stick him a second time. He grabbed Flat-Eye's wrist, yanking the Chinaman's arm away, trying to keep from getting the business end of yet another pick-sticker jammed into him. Twice in one day was enough. The Chinaman's arm was slippery with blood—Ferdie realized with horror that it was his own. He lost his grip, and Flat-Eye used the advantage. He rolled on top of Ferdie, knife raised up impossibly high as a prelude to sinking into Ferdie's gut.

Ferdie, spurting blood from two wounds, gouged his fingers in the Chinaman's eyes. Flat-Eye howled in pain and rage, which gave Ferdie just enough time to knock the knife out of the Chinaman's hand. Ferdie scrambled for it and Flat-Eye was all over him, saying over and over, with obvious delight, "Fucky fucky. Fucky fucky."

Ferdie reached for the knife, and Flat-Eye tried to stop him. Ferdie jabbed an elbow into Flat-Eye's chin, knocking him away. Ferdie grabbed the knife and rolled onto his back just as Flat-Eye came at him again. Ferdie thrust the knife upward. Flat-Eye chose that moment to land on Ferdie, and the knife took him square in the belly, up to the hilt. Flat-Eye gave out a groan and died on top of him. Ferdie pushed him away, covered in blood.

"Fucky fucky you," Ferdie said to the Chinaman's lifeless body.

Fargo, meanwhile, fired at Lonegan and wished he had at least two more hands. Corny's flailing had grown a little weaker. His neck would break in seconds. Fargo aimed and fired at the tree, hitting the rope where it was wrapped around the tree limb, snapping it. Corny flopped to the ground three yards from Tucker's body, and didn't move.

There were two bullets left in the chamber of the Colt. His own, still sitting peacefully in his holster, was too far away to do him any good now. Trying for it would be suicide.

Neither Lonegan nor Al Bridge, on the other hand, seemed to be having any ammunition supply problems. Bullets pinged off the rocks and around Fargo. Lonegan dashed out from behind the live oak, moving as if his ass was on fire. Fargo took careful aim and fired a shot just as Lonegan somersaulted behind a pile of rocks that had once been a stone hearth barbeque. There was just enough of him visible for a clean shot. Fargo took it and missed, cursing a blue streak at his luck, which seemed to be deserting him. At the same time, he heard another shot boom from inside the cabin. The shot found its mark; Fargo felt the bullet tear into his upper arm. The game was all but over now.

"He's hit, Deke," Bridge said from inside the cabin. "All clear."

Simultaneously, Bridge stepped out of the cabin, clutching his Sharps rifle. Lonegan came out from behind the pile of rocks. Corny still lay motionless on the ground, and Fargo feared the worst. The poor dumb bastards had paid him to show them a good time, and he'd gotten them both killed.

"A real purdy sight, ain't they, Deke?" Bridge asked.

"Ain't never looked better," Lonegan said. He gave Corny a couple of hard kicks in the side, knocking him onto his back. He saw no signs of breathing. "This one's had it," he said.

"Yeah, well, this one ain't," Bridge said, and walked over to where Fargo was laying. He was bleeding from the wound in his arm.

"You a religious man?" Bridge asked. "Cause if you are, you best prepare to meet your Maker."

"You go to Hell," Fargo said.

Bridge cocked the Sharps and popped one bullet into it. He aimed at Fargo's head and said, "You first."

Atop the ridge, Ferdie, weaving from dizziness and light-headed from the loss of blood, took extra careful aim and fired the Henry.

Fargo shut his eyes as the shot rang out, and felt nothing. The shot seemed to have come from the wrong direction. Fargo opened one eye. Al Bridge sported a nice big hole in his chest, an inch under the heart but close enough. Blood spurted from the wound.

Up on the ridge, the kick from the Henry once more knocked Ferdie over. Weakened now, he pitched forward and tumbled down the ridge, bouncing off mesquite and rocks, until coming to rest at the bottom in a crumpled heap.

"Think . . . I'm . . . shot . . ." Bridge said, miraculously still standing. The Sharps slipped from his fingers, clattering onto the ground. All the flying dust kicked up by the shooting clogged Fargo's nose. He let out a strong, healthy sneeze. Al Bridge toppled to the ground, mercifully dead. Tucked inside his holster was a spanking, brand new six-shot, single-action New Model Army pistol with rounded barrel and trigger guard.

Fargo went for it, but Lonegan got there first.

"Not so fast, sidewinder," Lonegan said, plucking the gun from the holster. He walked over to Ferdie, who was fighting to stay conscious, and for breath.

"Some pretty fair shootin', rugrats," Lonegan said. "Old Al Bridge is tough, been with me a long time. But what the hell, I'll just get me some new friends."

"Excuse me, Mr. Lonegan?" Corny spoke up softly from behind him.

Lonegan wheeled around. Corny was on his knees, holding Tucker's pistol. He fired, hitting Lonegan in the belly. Lonegan fired back a beat later. The bullet ricocheted off a rock and struck Corny squarely in the ass. Corny went face down in the dirt, but managed to get off another shot, this time hitting Lonegan in the groin.

Lonegan dropped his gun, and staggered around in some insane dance of death, shouting, "He killed me, the little shitbird killed me!" Blood seeped from his wounds.

"You go to hell, lard-ass," Corny said, and shot him again. He missed, but it mattered little. Lonegan sat down hard and fell over. He breathed his last and became still.

Corny looked over at Fargo and said, "You always said it was impolite to shoot someone in the back, so I didn't."

"Good boy," Fargo said.

Corny rolled up into a little ball and went unconscious.

Ferdie was hurt the worst. The hole in his leg wasn't too bad—the bullet had luckily passed clear through. The knife wound appeared to be more serious; it was deeper than was healthy. He'd also lost a lot of blood. His breathing was thin and reedy. Corny had a bullet in his rump and an ugly red rope-burn around his neck, this in addition to the wound he'd gotten back in Del Rio.

Somehow, Fargo, with only one good arm, managed to get them slung onto the horses and back to San Carlos. There was nothing even closely resembling a doctor, but the older Mexican women there knew only too well how to deal with gunshot and knife wounds. Fargo and his party were bloody messes, but the wrinkly brown women had seen worse.

Beds were set up in the crumbling church, and all the good people of San Carlos pitched in to help the brave *gringos Americanos* who had killed the evil Deke Lonegan, whose boys had evidently been terrorizing the helpless peasants—the younger women, most notably—of the small Mexican town.

"May soul roast in Hell," said an ancient, white-haired man, in broken English.

When he was able to get up and around a day later, Fargo went back to the cabin and retrieved what was left of the stolen bank money, almost five thousand dollars. It was probably a lot less than Lonegan and his pals had taken out of the bank, but it was better than nothing.

After a couple of days, thanks to the excellent care and feeding by the women of San Carlos, Ferdie and Corny were improving. They'd live, but they weren't going to be very pretty for a spell. Ferdie was still as weak as a kitten, but some of his color had returned, and he was taking solid food, mostly beans and rice and an occasional chunk of goat meat.

Two days later, a gringo rode into the small village. He was well dressed but dusty, as though he'd been on the trail for some time. His name was Mackley Green and he was with the Pinkertons, out of the Dallas office. As Ferdie and Corny slept that evening, Fargo and Mackley Green shared a bottle of tequila.

Green told Fargo, "Their daddies hired us to keep an eye on them. Trailed y'all as far as Del Rio, then you dropped off the map. Wasn't too hard pickin' up your scent, though—you fellers cut a pretty wide swath through South Texas."

"They ain't the same boys they were when they arrived here a week ago," Fargo agreed.

"Those boys really took out the Lonegan Gang?" Green asked incredulously. "Between the Rangers and us Pinkertons, we been trying to track them down for near four years. And you're tellin' me you and a couple of greenhorn kids from back East did the job your ownselves?"

"Wasn't me, just them greenhorns from back East," Fargo said. "Mr. Wallington and Mr. Fisk. They did the actual killin', not me. And got their asses shot up in the process." Fargo shook his head, remembering. "Never thought they had it in 'em."

"There was a price on their heads," Green said. "Almost nine thousand dollars."

Fargo laughed, but it came out a grunt. He said, "Should be just enough to pay for a couple of good lawyers."

"Lawyers?" Green asked.

"Well, yeah," Fargo said. "We still got to stand trial for robbin' that bank back in San Angelo, not to mention all those good people gettin' killed."

"You and your friends didn't rob that bank, Deke Lonegan did," Green said. "You didn't kill anybody. Lonegan and his boys pulled those triggers. We've known that all along."

"But we were robbing the bank," Fargo said. "Well, maybe not for money, but we tried all the same, and it was just our bad luck Deke Lonegan and his merry band of murderers picked the same time. What are the odds of that, Mr. Green? It's hog wild, but it's the truth."

"We know it is, and the Rangers know it," Green said. "You and Misters Wallingford and Fisk were never suspects."

"We weren't?"

"Shit no," Green said, and helped himself to more tequila. "A woman named Miss Nellie, runs a cathouse, volunteered what you'd told her about the so-called robbery. Rangers also found the bags of washers, I hear tell."

"But we ran!" Fargo said, getting a little angry. "After that robbery, we ran like three farts in a tailwind. Don't that make us guilty by association, or something?"

"Between you and me, Mr. Fargo, I'd have lit out too, all things being equal. If I'd been there first-hand, I don't think I would've believed your wild yarn. You were smart to run, mister."

"To hell," Fargo said. "We went to hell six ways from Sunday to get that money back, killin' Deke Lonegan and his men to boot, and now you're telling me we didn't have to?"

"Sounds about right," Green said, adding softly, "and don't forget this, neither, Mr. Fargo: We're the Pinkertons, and we know who you are."

"Is that a fact?"

"Your reputation is solid, Fargo," Green said. "We know you ain't in the habit of slaughtering innocent people," Green said. "The ones you did kill, well, they either had prices on their heads, or they damn well should have."

"Well, I'll be goddamned," Fargo said. "For nothing. We did it for nothing."

"Not for nothing, Fargo," Green said. "If what you say is true, then the world's a better place without Deke Lonegan and his ilk. You understand, of course, that the bodies'll need to be identified before the reward can be paid."

"Talk to the people here in the village," Fargo said. "They planted 'em, we didn't have the strength. If it was up to me, the buzzards were welcome to them."

"We'll have half a dozen men down here day after tomorrow to take them kids to Dallas and put 'em on a train," Green said. "Their daddies are gonna want them back pronto when we file our report about the shoot-out here. Rich men don't cotton to seeing their sons all shot to shit in Mexico."

"Those kids have shed blood, they don't need any escort," Fargo said.

"The Pinkertons don't agree with you, sir. We'll handle it our way."

"Let's hear what our friends have to say, why don't we?"

Fargo suggested. "They're strong enough to voice their opinions."

Fargo took Green to see his wounded troops. In the end, it was agreed that Green and his men could accompany them, but at a distance. Ferdie and Corny also wanted the nine thousand dollars.

The stagecoach from Eagle Pass, the one that would take Ferdie and Corny back to Dallas, was two hours late, which was unusual. It was usually five hours late, or so they were told.

True to their word, the Pinkertons trailed behind Fargo and his friends on the journey from San Carlos to Crystal City. It was fifty or so miles out of the way, but Mackley Green strongly advised them to steer clear of Del Rio. Though Marshal Lattigo Tucker was corrupt clear down to his socks, he still had friends there who would be more than happy to ventilate those that were responsible for his untimely demise. That Ferdie and Corny didn't actually kill him at all was of no consequence.

It was a two-and-half day ride by coach to Dallas. There they would catch one of the six trains that would get them home.

They were standing outside of the Livermore Cafe, waiting. Ferdie had two layers of bandages wrapped around his middle. His leg was likewise wrapped up pretty good, and he would be forced to walk with a crutch for the next month. Corny had his left arm in sling, and both of his eyes were blackened from beatings administered by the Lonegan Gang. A bandage was tightly wrapped around his head, and the rope burn on his neck had yet to fade. He walked stiffly, making it a little easier on his butt. Both of their faces were covered with cuts and bruises.

"Shot in the ass," he said. "Could anything be more humiliating?"

When the stagecoach finally did show signs of arriving, Fargo said to them, "I hope you both got your money's worth."

"Oh, I would say so," Ferdie said.

"Me, too," Corny chimed in.

"We don't have to go home, you know," Ferdie said. "In fact, Corny and I were sort of thinking about staying around. Not counting the trip back, we still have six weeks before we're due in New York. And with that nine thousand dollars due us on the bounty—"

"And I said I'd wire the money to you back East," Fargo interrupted. "You boys are going home."

"But you'll keep half of it for yourself, like we agreed, right?" Corny asked. "We owe you that much. The rest will cover what Mr. Lonegan stole from the bank."

"You don't have to do that," Fargo said. "You boys earned that reward money."

"Tom Cash had a family, we heard," Ferdie said. "They likely need it much more than we do. You'll see that they get it, won't you, Skye?"

"They'll get it," Fargo said.

The stagecoach thundered into town, stopping in front of the cafe. The drivers jumped down and dashed off to take a leak, leaving the passengers to fend for themselves.

"Well, I guess this is it, gentlemen. Thanks for saving my life," Fargo said.

"Thanks for saving ours," Corny said.

They had come here as boys and were going home as men. Killing had that effect. "You done real good, partners. I'm proud of you both."

Among the passengers climbing off the muddy stagecoach was a woman in a red gingham dress with matching hat and parasol. She had a nice figure and a nice, round bottom. When she turned around, it took Corny a second to recognize her. It was Olive.

She took one look at the motley bunch and her face turned beet red in anger. She stomped over to them, and she didn't look happy.

"Olive," Fargo said pleasantly. "What brings you to Crystal City?"

"A stagecoach," she said. "Del Rio was getting old real fast. Figured on setting up shop here."

Corny said, happily, "You're not dead."

"You're damn right I'm not, no thanks to you," she snapped. "You knocked me senseless, you dumb cluck. Had a lump on my head the size of a billiard ball for a whole week."

"I'm sorry," Corny said.

"I'm willing to forgive and forget, seeing how y'all killed

Deke Lonegan," she said. She noticed their new carpetbags and said, "You're leaving?"

"I guess so," Corny said.

"Gonna write about me in your diary?" she asked.

"Well, of course I will—" Corny's eyes widened. He said. "My diary! I lost it."

"No you didn't," Olive said. She reached into one of her bags and pulled out Corny's dog-eared notebook. "Found it under the bed. Don't ask me how it got there."

"I can't thank you enough," Corny said, clutching it. To Ferdie he said, "If you tell anyone I keep a diary, partner, you'll be picking lead out of your belly."

"I stand warned, partner," Ferdie said.

"I really must be going," Olive said, and picked up her bags. "You ever get back to Crystal City, you be sure and look me up."

"May I carry your bags for you?" Corny asked sheepishly.

"That would be—" Olive started to say.

"You ain't the time, Casanova," Fargo said. "You got to get your bony ass on that stage. Both of you. I'll carry the lady's bags."

Reluctantly, Ferdie and Corny boarded the coach, though with some difficulty due to their wounds. Fargo shook their hands. "Take care, amigos. You get out this way again, do me a big favor and don't look me up."

"Goodbye, Mr. Fargo," Corny said. "In spite of everything, we really did have a good time. Didn't we, Ferdie?"

"I guess we did," Ferdie said. "We really do thank you for all the trouble you got us into."

"Wasn't anything much," Fargo said. "No thanks necessary."

"Where are you going now?" Ferdie asked.

"I'll tell you when I get there," Fargo said.

The driver and the shotgun rider returned and climbed on. Other than a fat, sweaty drummer with a sample case, Ferdie and Corny were the only passengers.

Fargo gave them a wave as the stagecoach lurched down the main street, and disappeared around a bend and was gone from sight.

"I'm waiting, Skye," Olive said.

Fargo grabbed her bags and they started off toward the

only hotel in town. Finally, he turned to her and said, "Nice guys . . . but I hope I never lay eyes on them again."

Bouncing along in the stage, Ferdie said to Corny, "Sure is an attractive lady, that Olive. Don't you think?"

"I hate it when you read my mind," Corny said glumly.

"Be a shame to leave her to the likes of Skye Fargo," Ferdie said.

"Yeah, I guess it would," Corny said. "Did you have something in mind?"

"That Pinkerton man, Mr. Green, he gave us each a hundred dollars for train tickets and eats, right?"

"So?"

"That money could hold us until the reward comes through," Ferdie said. "Hell, Corny, we tighten our belts, it could last us all summer."

"Sure," Corny said, excited. "Our old men gave us the summer, Goddammit, and that's what we're going to take."

Ferdie told the stagecoach driver to stop. They threw their carpetbags into the sweltering South Texas, July afternoon and helped each other off the coach. The driver, a gray-haired, grizzled old coot, asked them, "You sure you wanna do this? It's almost two miles back to town, and you boys ain't in the best of condition."

"We'll be just dandy, thanks," Corny told him. "Be on your way."

"Suit yourselves," the driver said, and off he went, kicking up dust. Corny handed his friend the crutch. Together they began the slow trek back to Crystal City, two battered but determined young men with two hundred dollars between them. The sun was setting now. Maybe it would cool things down.

Corny said to his friend, "I can't wait to see the look on Fargo's face when we come back. Think he'll be glad to see us?"

"Not a chance," Ferdie said. "I can't wait."

LOOKING FORWARD!

The following is the opening section from the next novel in the exciting *Trailsman* series from Signet:

THE TRAILSMAN # 225

PRAIRIE FIRESTORM

*1860—where the great untamed plains
of the New Land brought out both the best
and the worst in men, and proved
that savagery can wear many faces. . . .*

The town outside the window had a name: Sandstone.

The girl in the bed beside him had a name: Betsy.

Strangely enough, they had certain similarities.

The town was one of those he called "not quite" towns. Not quite close enough to a wagon trail to grow and prosper, not quite large enough to have a sheriff, not quite in a location good enough to attract people to settle in and around it, and not quite able to do more than simply exist. There were many like it scattered along the edge of the Great Plains.

Betsy was a "not quite" girl as well; not quite pretty, not quite voluptuous, not quite ambitious enough to pick up sticks and move on. Yet she had been pleasant enough, warm and willing, and it had been a hot, hard trip breaking trail for Ted Olson's herd all the way from the Texas panhandle. When he'd finished, he'd ridden on to Sandstone only because Miles Davis had asked him to meet there. When he reached Sandstone, Betsy had been waiting tables at the saloon and she had been sweet and one thing led to another, as it often does. That had been three days ago, much of it spent in Betsy's bed in the small house not far from the saloon. He rose quietly, his lake-blue eyes peering through the window as another day rose. A tiny furrow touched his brow. Miles was late and it wasn't like General Miles Davis, U.S. Cavalry, to be late.

Skye Fargo turned from the window as Betsy stirred, opening soft-brown eyes, sitting up and wrapping herself around him at once. "Mmmmmmmm, I like it in the morning," she whispered, her breasts pressing into him, her muscled thighs lifting to wrap around him. She lay back, pulling him down with her. Betsy had a warm, tingling skin that could start an instant, tactile fire to which he instantly responded. His fingers painted an invisible line across her shallow breasts, pausing to circle her small, dark-red nipples set against larger matching circles. Betsy groaned happily. He continued to wander downward, over her small but puffy little belly, down to the curly down that she pushed upwards at once to meet his touch.

"Oh, God, oh yes," Betsy murmured, her soft moans illicited by the touch of his hand, moans that grew louder as he moved lower, taking on a new note of pleasure when he reached the dark apex. Betsy was a creature of instant wanting. There was no coyness to her, no games, and it was perhaps that plain, unvarnished sincerity that gave her a special quality; a simple, uncluttered sexuality that had its own power. When her soft murmurings grew into rising groans, he felt her eager warmth around him, lifting her entire body to move in sublime harmony with his, finally finding that too-short moment of ecstatic intensity that was forever the same and forever new.

She screamed her pleasure and satisfaction and her body jiggled against him until finally she sank back onto the bed, spent and satiated, her arms and legs still clinging to him.

Only when her breath returned in full did she relax her limbs. Her soft brown eyes peered at him, the hint of a private thought edging her lips. "Maybe your friend isn't coming. I'd like that," she murmured smugly.

"If he doesn't, he'll send somebody," Fargo said confidently. As an officer in the United States Cavalry, Miles Davis's position demanded no less. His personal code of behavior wouldn't let him do otherwise. Fargo lay back and Betsy bent her body over him.

"There's always a first time," she said, unwilling to relinquish hope. "You could stay on then," she added, not that she needed to. He smiled but knew he'd not be staying. A list of jobs awaited him, each needing someone who could find what others missed, who could read what others only saw, each needing the Trailsman's knowledge and special gifts. Even if Betsy were the most beautiful woman in the world, he'd not stay. His world, his life, his love of searching the land, still beckoned him with an undiminished song. And despite what she wanted, Betsy knew that. Perhaps that was why she wanted so much so often. Storing memories was the next best thing to reality.

Her soft-fleshed body slid against him again and in moments the room once more echoed her soft moans. The sun was in the mid-morning sky when Betsy made breakfast, wearing only a thin, loose shift. Fargo dressed, and had just finished his coffee when the sound of hooves rumbled through the room from outside. Betsy went with him to the window and gazed out at the double column of blue and gold uniforms astride sturdy, dark-sable mounts. A second lieutenant led the column, Fargo noted. "Told you Miles would send somebody," he commented.

"Jeez, he always send a hundred troopers?" Betsy murmured.

"No," Fargo admitted as Betsy clung to him.

"Will you come back?" she asked.

"I'll try," he said, tasting her kiss before hurrying from the house. The troopers had halted at the stage depot as Miles had arranged. Fargo strode up to the second lieutenant. "Skye Fargo," he introduced himself.

"Lieutenant Boomer," the young officer said.

Fargo's eyes swept the long column. "I don't see General Davis," he said.

"He's at the field camp. We're on our way there. You're to come with us," the officer said.

"I'll get my horse." Fargo nodded, and hurried to the town stable and retrieved the Ovaro, its jet-black fore-and-rear quarters and its pure-white midsection glistening in the sun. He swung in beside the lieutenant as the officer waved the column forward. "Why the whole platoon?" he questioned.

"We're joining the others at the field command. We'll all be going on together," the lieutenant said.

"Going on where?" Fargo questioned.

"The general will tell you that if he wants to," Boomer said and Fargo smiled. Never give information you're not authorized to give, part of every officer's manual. He rode on in silence as he wondered what had made the general send for him this time. He knew one thing: Miles never called him in for something trivial. He'd worked enough with Miles Davis to know that. Lieutenant Boomer kept the double-column at a trot, but it was already mid-afternoon when they reached a dip in the land, and Fargo saw the neat rows of pup tents that marked a field camp, horses tethered along both sides of the tents. Miles Davis emerged from the larger, command tent as Fargo drew to a halt, his thick, silver-white hair topping a handsome, still-youthful face.

"Been waiting, old friend," the general boomed. "How are you?"

"Can't complain," Fargo said, grasping the general's outstretched hand, then followed his tall, straight figure into the tent. Sinking into a canvas-backed chair, Fargo watched the General allow a wry smile to edge his lips. "What're you cooking for me to taste?" Fargo said.

"Maybe I just wanted to see you. You're growing cynical," the general said.

"I'm growing smart," Fargo replied. "You've your whole damn command in a field camp. Why?"

"They're moving me," Miles Davis said unhappily. "Want me to take charge of the Department of Texas. They want me on-hands there, for a while, at least."

Fargo's brows rose. "That's a lot of territory, all of Texas, New Mexico, the Oklahoma Indian territory—along with the Comanche, the Chiricahua Apache, the Jicarillo, and all those wild Comanchero bands. Why the move?"

"There's increasing talk of war between the states. The army's pulling out all the men it can spare. They need someone who knows how to run a lot of land with a handful of men," Miles said.

"Which is pretty much what you've been doing for years up here," Fargo put in.

"I'll still technically be in command of the plains territories, but it'll be mostly in name only. I won't be really able to know what's going on and that's what's bothering me," Miles Davis said.

"How do I figure in this?" Fargo questioned.

"I'm worried about what I'm leaving behind, mainly General Robert Carlton," the general said and again Fargo's brows lifted.

"You're worried about one of your own people?"

"General Carlton's been running things but I've always held a tight rein on him. I won't be able to do that, now. Carlton's a desk general, never been a field commander, but with his own personal connections and the Army's need for filling posts, he was appointed. He doesn't know the plains, doesn't understand the dynamics that go on there. He's voiced ideas on how to keep control of the tribes that scare me."

"You outrank him. Why didn't you just slap him down?" Fargo asked.

"He hasn't done anything to allow me do that. It's all been in the area of talk and memorandums, suggestion and opinions. He's clever with words. He kept putting me in the position that if I disagreed with him, I'd sound as though I didn't want to take action against the Indians. But now with my moving south, he'll have a free hand. I need someone I can trust to keep an eye on General Carlton and keep me informed, at least until I can get back there."

"That's me?" Fargo frowned.

"Bullseye," Miles Davis said.

"No general, especially one such as him, is going to take orders from a civilian," Fargo said.

"I don't expect that. I want you on the scene to evaluate with your own eyes, in the way only you can, and report back to me. I'll have two couriers stationed in Elbow Flats. You can use them to get reports back to me."

"Why don't you just remove him?" Fargo queried.

"I can't, not without real proof. Right now I've a lot of uneasiness but no real evidence of anything to go with it. I've been looking over his shoulder up until now and he's had to be careful. But Carlton's the kind of man to let personal ambition destroy judgment. You know the army's full of small dictators. It's only when they get into a position where they can do some real harm that they became dangerous. Because of my orders to move south, Carlton's been put into that position. That's why I need your eyes and ears," Miles Davis said as he opened a file folder and drew out a letter on official army stationary. "You'll take this with you," he said and read the letter aloud.

"Brigadier General Robert Carlton, USA:
   This will introduce Mr. Skye Fargo, who is widely known as the Trailsman. He has served the army on numerous delicate assignments. I have always found his special knowledge, instincts and experience to be of tremendous value. I hope you will find him equally helpful. Please extend him every courtesy.
                   Major General Miles Davis, USA"

Fargo smiled. "That's sending a message. Subtly. You think he'll take it?" he asked.

"Anybody's guess," the general shrugged. "But he'll have to be careful." He rose as he handed the letter to Fargo, and Fargo pushed to his feet with him, walking beside him from the tent. "Same rates as always, old friend," the general said. "More than the army pays any other civilian."

"And they should," Fargo laughed as they reached the Ovaro.

"Won't argue that. Good luck," Miles Davis said as Fargo swung onto the horse. "Remember, those two couriers will be at Elbow Flat just for you."

"How long are you going to be holding things down south?" Fargo questioned.

"Until Washington decides different. I'll be headquartered at Fort Ransom, Oklahoma territory, but I'll be moving around. The two couriers will be kept informed where I'll be," Miles said, and raised his hand in salute as Fargo sent the Ovaro off into a canter. Fargo kept the horse at a good pace in the later afternoon haze, headed north and west, holding steady until night descended. He found a place to stretch out in a cluster of black walnut and lay awake on his bedroll. The distant cry of timberwolves circled through the night and he smiled as he saw a mental picture of the land that lay in the darkness ahead of him.

The great plains were a vast and untamed area, a place of contrasts; beauty and cruelty, richness and sparseness, a place that could offer great rewards and provide a sudden death. The great plains were an area that teemed with life of every kind, from the tiny vole to the mighty buffalo, from the soft chatter of the goldfinch to the scream of the golden eagle. It harbored every kind of gift a man could want, and every kind of danger a man could face. But this vast land was made of balances, every creature playing its role, from predator to prey, every tree, bush, flower and creature in its place, all part of the vast balance that was the great plains.

Only man had come to intrude on that balance, disturbing that ecological equilibrium. And not all men, Fargo grunted. The red man lived inside the vast balance, had become part of it, until now he, too, had torn himself out of his place. Fargo closed his eyes, letting sleep wash over him as he thought about the unknown dangers that lay waiting when the natural order of things was upset.

When the new day woke him, Fargo found a stream and washed and was in the saddle when the sun blanketed the land, the day dry and hot. It was under a noonday sky when he halted the gleaming Ovaro. He stayed in the saddle as his eyes peered out across the great plains that stretched before him. It was not unlike standing at the edge of an immense sea of green, he reflected, beckoning yet silently warning. I can be yours, it murmured, if you are wise enough and strong enough. I can be yours, or I can make you mine.

Elbow Flats lay some fifty miles west of the edge of the plains. Nestled at the lower edge of the great prairie, the town played host to plenty of dreamers who needed to take on fresh supplies before setting off across the heat of the plains. From Elbow Flats, wagon trains could roll northward to the Santa Fe Trail, the Oregon Trail, and the Mormon Trail. On these trails, most would push westward, some to connect with the Old Spanish Trail, the Gila River Trail and the California Trail. But there were many who'd push west forging their own trails, convinced there were better places to find than following the old trails. Sometimes they were right. Sometimes they were wrong. And too often, being wrong meant being dead.

But he'd get to Elbow Flats later, Fargo told himself. His goals were not limited to towns, nor to wagon trains. His goals included both and a lot more and he sent the Ovaro forward onto the vast plains, a land he knew perhaps better than any other man, and he allowed a wry smile at how little that really meant. His gaze swept the prairie as he rode, not hurrying. Legislators and local governments created states and territories and gave names to their creations. But the army paid little heed to that and divided the plains—indeed, all of the new western lands—into its own divisions. They drew their own boundaries based on their own strengths and estimates.

The lower plains they titled the Department of the Missouri. That division took in not only Missouri, but Illinois, Kansas, Colorado, and Utah; an area the Pawnee, the Shoshoni, the Kiowa, the Utes, the Missouris, and the Osage also called their own. Above that, the army created the Department of the Platte, anchored by the Platte River.

Here they took in Iowa, Nebraska and Wyoming. In these states and territories, the Cheyenne and the Arapaho ruled the plains. Above that, reaching northward, the Army established the Department of Dakota, which covered the entire northern plains territories of North and South Dakota, Minnesota, Montana, and on up to the Canadian border. In these northern plains states the Sioux and the Crow were the most powerful of the tribes, with the Poncas, Assiniboins and the Nez Perce close behind, then the Sauk and Fox.

This was the geography the army had set for itself, defining the expansive tinderbox of delicate balances. It was no place for the inexperienced or the amateur, and no place for fools or ambitious egotists. Fargo let grim thoughts slide into a corner of his mind as he rode on, paused to pick up a torn piece of armband. Kiowa, he noted by the design and he'd gone on for another half-hour or so when, moving just inside a long line of cottonwoods, he suddenly felt the ground vibrate with the pounding of hooves. The Ovaro felt it at the same moment and immediately tensed. Fargo stroked its jet-black neck as he swung from the saddle and knelt one knee on the ground, letting every inch of his body become a sounding board.

Not Indian ponies, he muttered as he absorbed the thundering sound. This was the pounding of shod hooves. His ears picked up the next sound, that of rein chains, then the slap of leather chaps against horseflesh. He continued to pick up vibrations and this time they told him who the riders were that rode hard toward where he waited. It was not a mixture of individual riders, each setting their own pace and gait for their horses. These horses moved at a steady, uniform pace, almost in rhythm. "Cavalry," he grunted and climbed back onto the Ovaro. As he peered out through the trees, only minutes later the blue and gold uniforms appeared in the sunlight, a platoon led by a lieutenant. Fargo watched the troopers pass by, noting the letter B on their small, triangular platoon banner.

They continued to ride hard, almost at a gallop, plainly with a goal in mind. Staying in the trees, Fargo moved the

Ovaro forward and followed. The platoon had outdistanced him but the column of dust they sent up was easy enough to follow. Only a few minutes more passed when a fusillade of shots split the air, all the heavy explosions of army carbines. Fargo put the pinto into a canter and hurried forward inside the cottonwoods, slowing when he saw the scene unfolding on the open land to his left. The platoon was pouring fire into a small Kiowa camp. Fargo's quick glance saw only squaws, naked children and a half-dozen old men in the camp. The women, some clutching children in their arms, tried to flee and Fargo scowled in disbelief as the troopers poured lead into them.

An old man with long, gray, straggly hair tried to fire his bow and was cut down by a hail of bullets. A young woman fell with her arms still wrapped around her child. Fargo, the frown digging deep into his forehead, reached back and drew the big Henry from its saddlecase, and brought the rifle to his shoulder. He'd no desire to shoot U.S. cavalrymen but a massacre was a massacre, no matter who was doing it. He swung the rifle at two troopers riding down a young squaw with an infant in her arms. Using his superb marksmanship and the accuracy of the big Henry, he fired and one trooper's hat flew from his head. Another shot sent the second trooper's carbine spinning from his hands. Both soldiers reined up at once, surprise flooding their faces as they wheeled their mounts and stared toward the trees.

Fargo shifted position in the cottonwoods, firing at a trooper about to bring his carbine down on an old woman. His gun fell from his grip as Fargo's shot creased the top of his forearm. Fargo shifted position in the trees again, and fired. Another trooper's saber flew from his belt. Fargo saw the soldiers turning, surprised, and confused, the young lieutenant moving forward to peer into the trees. It was enough time for the remaining squaws, children and old men to reach a stand of shadbush behind the camp, and Fargo waited as the lieutenant drew his troop back to form a line that faced the cottonwoods. They waited, rifles ready to lay down a barrage, plainly expecting to face a Kiowa charge.

Fargo slid the Henry back into its saddlecase and slowly walked the Ovaro out of the cottonwoods. He let the horse amble toward the line of troopers and the lieutenant moved forward to meet him. Fargo saw a young face, dark hair poking from under his cap, dark-brown eyes, and a face that was probably always serious, he guessed. It was clean-shaven, with a young man's skin that held no marks of age. The army was commissioning them younger and younger, Fargo grunted silently. "You see any Kiowa in those cottonwoods?" the lieutenant frowned.

"Can't say that I did," Fargo answered.

"Maybe only three or four of them. You see any signs of anyone near where you were?" the lieutenant said.

"There wasn't anybody in those cottonwoods except me," Fargo said. "I did the shooting."

The lieutenant's mouth fell open as he stared back at Fargo. "You?" he said, finally, swallowing hard.

"That's right. Just little old me," Fargo said blandly.

The lieutenant drew his indignation around himself. "Why in hell were you shooting soldiers of the United States cavalry, mister?" he flung out.

"I didn't really shoot at your boys. You'd have six dead troopers if I'd done that," Fargo chided.

"Dammit, you interfered in an army attack," the lieutenant snapped.

"That was no attack. That was a massacre. There's a difference. I don't sit by for massacres, whether it's the Kiowa or the cavalry doing them," Fargo returned.

"Massacre is your word, mister. That doesn't make it so."

"I know a massacre when I see one. You were shooting down helpless squaws, children and old men. What would you call it?" Fargo said.

The lieutenant was either too honest or too young to hide the moment of discomfort from his face. "I'd call it following orders," he said. "Who are you, mister? Lieutenant Thomas Nickles asking, Third Regiment, Platoon B."

"Skye Fargo answering. Who's orders were you following?"

"My Commander's. General Robert Carlton," Lieutenant Nickles answered.

"I'd like to hear him explain ordering a massacre," Fargo remarked.

"I'm sure he'd enlighten you as to his orders."

"I'd like hearing that. Why don't I just follow you back?" Fargo suggested.

"The general's in the field. Pay him a visit in a few days. Fort Burns," Lieutenant Nickles said, letting his eyes bore into Fargo. "I don't know if I should just forget this," he muttered.

"Forget what?"

"You shooting at the U.S. Cavalry."

"I told you, I didn't shoot at your boys or they'd be dead," Fargo returned mildly.

"You came awfully close."

"That's called fancy shooting."

"Maybe too fancy. Maybe it was just dumb luck you didn't hit anybody. That kind of shooting's pretty hard to believe."

Fargo smiled as he drew the Henry from its case, and turned toward one of the tipis a few dozen yards away, aiming the rifle at the poles that rose up from the top of the tipi. "Pick a pole," he said.

"The center one," the lieutenant said, smiling doubtfully.

Fargo fired one shot, and the top of the center pole snapped off. "That help you believe?" he said laconically.

"Guess so," Nickles said, a touch of awe coming into his voice. "I've a feeling I'll be seeing you again, Fargo," he said as he turned his mount.

"Now, there's something else you can believe," Fargo said, and stayed in place to watch the lieutenant led platoon B northwest. When they were out of sight, he sent the pinto forward, passing the small Indian encampment and continuing on his way. Those hiding in the shadbush would return. What had taken place here would not be kept silent, he knew, and felt a stab of grim apprehension through him. He rode slowly, reaching a narrow river, and let the pinto drink as he refilled his canteen while a pair of golden eagles wheeled overhead. A mild breeze bent the long field of sweet clover that stretched out before him as he crossed the river and rode on into a thick stand of bur oak.

He climbed a low ridge heavily overgrown with oak and hackberry that just let him see into a long, shallow dip in the land, both sides heavy with dense foliage. Three deer, one a big buck, suddenly flashed across from him as they burst into the open. Fright was plain in their sudden, darting movements and seconds later, a half-dozen Indian ponies raced from the side of the rise. Fargo watched the six bucks send a hail of arrows at the three deer, every shaft hitting its mark. Moments later, the three deer lay lifeless on the ground. The six braves, one wearing a Kiowa armband, immediately leaped from their ponies and began loading their prizes onto their mounts, They laughed, exulted, their voices easily carrying to where Fargo watched from the trees across from them.

They were busy chattering as they secured the deer. "Plenty meat. Plenty good hides," one said. They were too busy to be aware of the brush that moved on the rise just behind them but Fargo's eyes caught the faint movement. He was first to see the blue uniformed riders that burst from the trees, laying down a withering barrage of gunfire as they did. The six braves leaped onto their ponies to flee but the attack was too fast, the hot lead too heavy. Only two managed to send their ponies racing away and only one of those disappeared into the thick foliage.

Fargo watched the cavalry platoon as it emerged fully onto the scene and noted the letter A on the platoon banner. He put the Ovaro into a trot, came out of the trees and went down the shallow hillside. A young lieutenant on his dark mount came forward. He was just as young as Nickles, Fargo saw, but with blond hair, a wispy mustache and light-blue eyes. He, too, tried to let serious formality mask his age. "Where'd you come from, mister?" he questioned.

"Back up there in the trees," Fargo said.

"The shooting bring you out?" the officer asked.

"No. I saw them bring down the deer," Fargo said, his glance sweeping across the slain braves. "They were a hunting party."

"I'm aware of that," the lieutenant said.

"Since when is the cavalry ambushing hunting parties?" Fargo asked.

"Since we got orders," the young officer said stiffly.

Fargo's glance went to the platoon banner. "Let me guess. Platoon A, Third Regiment," he slid out and the lieutenant's eyes widened.

"That's right," he said.

"Met up with platoon B. They were following orders, too. Mighty strange orders," Fargo commented.

"That's not for me nor Lieutenant Nickles to say," the officer answered. "Not for you, either, I'd say, mister."

"Sure it is. I can have an opinion. I'm not in the army. I'm not under orders," Fargo returned. "Name's, Fargo . . . Skye Fargo."

"Lieutenant Buzz Alderson," the young officer answered.

Fargo glanced at the silent figures on the ground again. "One of them got away, you know," he said and the lieutenant nodded. "He'll be saying plenty about this to his friends," Fargo mentioned.

"Oh, General Carlton expects there'll be a reaction," Alderson said a trifle smugly.

"He does, does he? And what kind of reaction does he expect?" Fargo pressed.

"Increased attacks on our patrols. The regiment's been fully prepared," the lieutenant said.

Fargo spit in disgust. "I'll tell you what the general ought to expect. He ought to expect the Indian not to do what's expected."

Alderson frowned. "I'll pass that on to him when I get the chance," he said.

"You do that, sonny, before it's too late," Fargo shot back. "Meanwhile, you might just go easy on following orders."

"I couldn't do that," the lieutenant said, visibly recoiling at the thought. "That'd be against regulations."

"Guess so, but they're regulations, not commandments. You could be saving a lot of lives."

The lieutenant frowned for a long moment. "I'll keep that in mind," he said dismissively and motioned to his troopers. Fargo watched as he led platoon A, Third Regiment U.S. Cavalry, from the little hollow of land. Turning the Ovaro, Fargo rode north and swore under his breath at the excellent job the army did of instilling its rules and principles. Miles Davis had more reason than he realized to be uneasy, Fargo grunted.

Riding slowly, Fargo set out to explore the lower plains, to read the signs and markings that would let him see what others failed to see. He rode north, then west, then back south, carefully searching the terrain. He probed the flat prairie, followed the rolling sagebrush, explored low hills with thick tree cover and dense ridges, went down deer trails that were used by a lot more creatures than just deer. He found pieces of wristbands, gauntlets, mocassins, broken arrows, all Kiowa except for a few Osage, and he was grateful for that. He glimpsed a few distant bands of near-naked riders and quickly took refuge, wanting no unecessary encounters.

When the day began to slip away, Fargo doubled back across the great plains that remained unchanging yet never the same. The day had been not unlike an unfinished sentence, its real meaning not what had been said but what hadn't been. He found a thick stand of shagbark hickory growing in moist soil beside a riverbank and set out his bedroll. A row of low hills rose up on the other side of the river and Fargo lay down and closed his eyes while a blanket of uncertainty stayed over him. Finally, he found sleep until the morning sun awoke him. He rolled up his gear, stepped to the river's edge with the Ovaro and an oath fell from his lips. Staring across the river, he saw four plumes of gray smoke rising up just beyond the row of low hills.

"Shit," he swore as he vaulted onto the horse, sending the pinto racing across the river, grateful for its shallowness. The terrible feeling had already curled into the pit of Fargo's stomach as he reached the other bank and charged up the incline.